THE LAST VOLUNTEER

THE LAST VOLUNTEER

The Doomsayer Journeys: Book 1

STEVE WETHERELL

Praise for The Doomsayer Journeys

"Wetherell writes like a modern Douglas Adams with a darker, more fantastical bent. The Doomsayer Journeys is stiff upper lip, prim and proper madness – like a nice cup of tea spiked with malicious nanobots and mescaline."

- Robert Brockway, *RX: A Tale of Electronegativity*

"There's far too little good comic fantasy out there. Wetherell's Doomsayer series is not only consistently funny all the way through, but it's a fast-paced, world-is-at-stake adventure too. Any fan of the genre will want to read this."

- Robert Bevan, *Critical Failures*

"I'm just going to say I gave this novel five stars. Why? If my wife has to ask me to stop reading because my laughing is disturbing her Candy Crush game, congrats, your book just earned five stars."

- Underground Book Reviews

"The thing I really like about editing Steve is I don't have to. He's naturally funny, concise, and maniacal. The thing I don't like about editing Steve is that I go home, and visions of his twisted imagination haunt my fevered dreams all through the night. So, you know, life is all about trade-offs."

- Brendan McGinley, *Man Cave Daily*

Dedicated to my wife and kids, who do a marvelous job of putting up with me.

Dedicated also to Stone Cold Iain. Cheers, man.

Prologue

There are some who say the outcome of events within the universes can be predicted by a mathematical equation so complex that not even the most highly evolved life form could begin to comprehend it. They speculate that if we were better able to follow a breadcrumb trail of chemistry and physics, we could trace events back through endless oceans of randominity and land on a tranquil beach of predictability and purpose. A certainty principle. A master pattern.

There are others who would call it naïve, optimistic, and even arrogant to assume the universes could be dumbed down to a recognizable shape, and that all perceived patterns are imposed by tiny minds trying to humanize oblivion, that chaos and unpredictability are the very nature of existence.

Both points of view have their merits, and the ensuing discussion between enlightened intellects of opposing opinions would doubtlessly make for a thrilling party. However, seeing as we have little time for high bar tabs and likely fistfights, we will bypass the philosophical route and head straight for the truth. Which is to say, there *is* an equation out there that defies the logic of the broadest human mind. In fact, there are many, but the one that interests us now is a formula, which if correctly understood, and if the right tools were present, could very well predict the exact course of a raindrop through a river. More importantly, however, the equation could tell us why the raindrop fell and what it was thinking at the time...

But most importantly of all, this equation is the very reason the raindrop *exists*. It is called the Universal Theory, and once you get to know it, it is far friendlier than you might imagine. It prefers to be called Ted...

1

Space, the Sentinel, and a Man Called Bip

Adjust your perspective to infinite. Now readjust to the averagely astronomical. And finally, set your sights on the merely gigantically enormous.

This is the planet Bersch, named ages ago after an astronomer who was enterprising enough to realize that no one had yet officially named the ground they were standing on. More practical people may have called their planet *Earth* or even *the ground*, but those people have little imagination.

Gigantically enormous is a particularly relevant term for this planet. Not on an ultraversal scale, or even on a universal scale, but as far as this particular solar system is concerned, Bersch is the big cheese. Burly planets swerve to avoid it and tiny moons hang in its orbit like barnacles on a warship. Even the resident gas giant is a touch intimidated.

If we concentrate and wait patiently, we can see a tiny twinkle of light curve around the planet's shoulder. Drift in closer and we can see that the light is reflected from a metal globe, a vessel of some kind, gliding along the blanket of stars like an ice skater's dream, hugging Bersch's exosphere like a shy child hugs its mother's legs.

A small plaque on the side of the vessel reads *S.S. Sentinel*.

Inside the globe it is dark, and cold too, with the kind of lifelessness that can only be found in lodgings abandoned by even the most molecular of tenants. From outside, dwarfed by the girth of Bersch, the vessel seemed tiny and toy-like. From the inside, however, perspective reveals that the *Sentinel* is verging on the cavernous. The long, wide decks are only partially illuminated by the soft, blue glow from the neighboring planet. The only noise is the calm hum of unseen machinery, a whispered lullaby for a slumbering starship.

On the inside wall on one of the many decks, staring out toward the vast vista of the galaxy, eight-foot-high pods stretch as far as the eye can see, their weighty, oval shapes tracking the curve of the globe's interior far into the distance. Each one emits a light into the gloom that, even though the pods are very close to us, seems to shine distantly through a thick fog. The only blemish on these otherwise smooth capsules is a small indentation that allows us to see inside. Inside this pod is a man. In the eerie stillness and translucent glow, he looks very peaceful...

Captain Finnegun dreamed. Technically, he shouldn't have been able to—the design of the chronostatic pod made the passing of centuries seem instantaneous to its occupants—but it is hard to contain a mind as broad and sharp as Captain Finnegun's.

He dreamed of penguins.

Slowly, but with an attitude toward urgency, a small light began to flick from red to green inside Finnegun's pod, harshly illuminating his clean-shaven face and giving him the appearance of a drunk in a disco. A gentle beeping noise began a soft but insistent monologue. It was the kind of beep that, while happy to be discreet at present, was promising to become a lot less patient and a lot more hostile if left unattended.

Years of the finest training had prepared Captain Finnegun for this exact moment. Even so, the first word he uttered as he awoke was a slightly confused, "Muh?"

With a suddenness seeming totally alien in the accustomed stillness, a green matrix of information began to scroll across the view port of Finnegun's pod, juddering and bleeping with urgent abandon.

Blinking the weariness from his eyes, the captain began to process the situation, and with a growing sense of horror he realized that nothing was as it should be.

Like a layabout's nightmare, Captain Finnegun's alarm had gone off nearly a millennium too early.

IT MIGHT BE prudent to point out that countless light years away from Bersch and the *Sentinel*, in a very different time and place, a civilization was standing—somewhat reluctantly—on the cusp of a new era of peace and prosperity. The assembled world leaders were standing sheepishly, like a group of boys caught fighting by an irate mother, shuffling their feet and avoiding one another's gaze. They were waiting for a countdown that would change everything they had ever known.

Since the beginning of their planet's history, there had been an ever-increasing love of war. Nations had never been more content than when bombing the living hell out of other nations. Oodles of political time and money went into merely looking for *excuses* to have a war. War was good. Everyone knew where they stood with war. Even if it was usually in a bomb shelter.

Now, though, it was becoming evident that in order for them to save their entire planet from being blown to pieces or rendered uninhabitable by radiation, something was going to have to be done. The Hundred-Year Arms Race had left the richer countries with more nuclear warheads than libraries, and the crippling financial consequences had forced them to sell on excess nuclear arms to smaller countries. This had all seemed like a good idea at the time, until one day everybody had come to the uneasy realization that nearly every country in the world, regardless of affiliation or financial power, had a more or less even supply of nuclear weaponry.

The slow and horrible understanding that one paranoid dictator or one political misunderstanding could result in a war that, while lasting only a few days, could blow up the world several times over began to sink into everybody's consciousness. And, thus, a referendum was proposed. And then discussed, and then scrapped, and then re-proposed and eventually—after five years of cold sweats and sleepless nights—was signed by every king, queen, president, and prime minister on the planet. It was a testament to the general mentality of this planet's people that the first thing politicians could all fully agree on was that the prospective fiery death of the entire population was not a good thing.

And so the world's government representatives stood rather dejectedly in the viewing area of the planet's largest spaceport, waiting for the pleasant electronic voice to finish the countdown that would signal the beginning of the biggest arms armistice in history. Billions watched through live satellite images as a fleet of more than a thousand rockets began to take off one by one, each of them laden with nuclear warheads and other payloads of destruction.

A cheer went up from the collective military and media personnel who had been assigned to chaperone the event. A few of the world leaders wiped a tear or two from their eyes; whether from relief and happiness or from a deep sense of loss no one could tell.

Destined for outer space, the rockets would undergo a few years of very careful maneuvering in orbit until they formed what the media had dubbed a "Massive Ball of Death." Further years would be spent welding these nuclear arms together to form the biggest man-made space artefact in the planet's history—a cluster of devastating weaponry just over a quarter the size of the planet's moon. Then, when all the weapons were in one comparatively safe place, a drive thruster would begin the bomb heap's steady journey toward a neighboring sun, where it was predicted it would explode with a minimal amount of fuss.

Hooray! Global security had advanced to the stage where only weapons of acceptable amounts of destruction were allowed, and the populace celebrated, glad that their problem now belonged to the seemingly uninhabited folds of outer space.

It says something about this civilization's nature that a few months after the nuclear arms had been sent on their merry way and it was reported that the Massive Ball of Death was a substantial way off its intended course, no one really cared much.

NOW LET'S get back to Bersch...

This is the northernmost continent of Bersch, although some people are reluctant to call it a continent as they're not sure whether building a continent out of ice isn't somehow cheating. But it is a continent nonetheless, and it rests like a white toupee on the crown of the bulbous world. Those who bother to learn about this chilled wasteland call it the Ice Plains because it is quite plain and made out of ice. And snow. There is also a lot of snow.

But mainly ice.

Nobody comes here; not just because it is a nasty place, but because it's a nasty place that is a bother to get to. No, nobody but the most bizarre and blubbery of creatures would inhabit this frosted stretch of soul-destroying wasteland. Therefore, it is quite surprising to see, nestled between two enormous mountains and teetering on the edge of a vertical cliff face, a quaint and surprisingly not ice-covered village.

The village comprises of several dozen triangular houses, some thatched, some tiled, but all made from wood, bar a large dome on the side of the village closest to the cliff, which appears to be made entirely of snow. In contrast to the surrounding icy harshness, the area around the village is a stretch of lush green farmland and forest that climbs the sides of the mountains and stops abruptly near the cliff edge. Comfortably cuddled from the raging elements, the village is reminiscent of an inverted snow globe.

This is the community of Kaneq: an oasis of spring in an eternal winter.

Hovering above and around the village is the reason Kaneq hasn't been eaten by a glacier or snowed under in mere seconds. A haze of nearly transparent heat creates an effective greenhouse wall, keeping the harsher elements out and letting only the weak sunshine in. It's quite interesting to watch it in action. For instance, if you could follow the direction of a particularly cruel gale as it winds through the Ice Plain mountains, past Old Bachalack and the Patient Mother, you'd be surprised to see it disperse in a flash of warmth as it hit the almost invisible barrier of shimmering heat that surrounds Kaneq. So, too, if you looked up at a vengeful snowstorm plummeting angrily from the sky, you might be impressed to see it transform, with a barely audible fizzing noise, into a gentle summer rain.

And so, thanks to the heatshield, it was on a warm spring day that Bip Plunkerton stepped back to look at his accomplishment. He removed his small half-moon glasses to see if what he was looking at was indeed actually there and not just some terrible trick of the light. A familiar sense of general disappointment crept over him. He turned to his friend Michaelmas, who was gaping at Bip's handiwork and looking as though he was attempting to cry and laugh at the same time. The portly man walked around the construction, scratching and shaking his balding head in a mixture of amazement and disgust.

"My wife is going to kill me," he finally said.

"Sorry, Michaelmas," said Bip. "I don't know what went wrong."

"No, no. You never does, but I think I can give you a hint, right?" Michaelmas walked back to Bip and put a burly arm over his smaller friend's shoulders. "What I said, right, was, 'Bip, if'n you're needing some practice with that psyence of yours, why don'ts you do us a favor and turn that crumbled old garden shed of mine into a conservatory for the wife, yes?' And you says, 'No problem, Michaelmas, my friend, it's the least I can do what with you being such a good friend and all.'"

Bip opened his mouth to speak. He wasn't sure that was exactly how the conversation had gone. His potential protest, however, was cut short by Michaelmas's litany.

"'Grand,' I says, and I lets you work yer hocus pocus on me garden shed—which me old granpappy built with his bare hands I might remind you—and what I get is not a conservatory, is it?"

Bip shook his head. There was no denying it. It definitely wasn't a conservatory.

"No, Bip, it isn't," continued Michaelmas. "What you did, instead of turning my garden shed into a conservatory likes I asked, you turned my garden shed—and my entire house—*into a bloody igloo!*"

Bip nodded in dumb agreement. Where before had stood a modest, hand-built, wooden house with a lovely thatched roof, now stood a rapidly melting igloo.

"Sorry, Michaelmas," he said. "I don't know how it happened."

"No, no you never does," said Michaelmas, running a hand across his suddenly tired-looking face. "I'm going to have a tough time explaining this one to the council. And then there's the wife." He groaned. There was always the wife.

Bip cleaned his glasses thoughtfully for a moment. "Well maybe I can try and—"

"Oh no!" interrupted Michaelmas. "No, no, no. Do me a favor and don't do me no more favors." He stopped and sighed, taking in the slump of Bip's shoulders and the defeat in his eye. "Look, mate, you've got talent and that's no lie, but you're going to need a hell of a lot of practice if'n you want to make your apprenticeship this year. The psyentists ain't just interested in talent—they need reliable men. Men who ain't suddenly going to turn their houses into igloos!"

"I know, I know," whined Bip. "I just don't know why this keeps happening to me. They're never going to let me be a psyentist if I can't even do a simple restructuring equation!" He kicked the igloo in frustration, resulting in a shower of ice.

"Tell you what, mate," said Michaelmas. "You bugger off and get some practice in, and I'll get a councilman or an elder to sort this out. I'll blame it on vandals or something."

Bip frowned. "What? Vandals turned your house into an igloo?"

"You got a better idea? No, vandals it was and vandals it shall be. A practical joke by some young upstart is what I'll tell 'em." He rubbed his moustache thoughtfully. "They've no reason not to believe me—stranger things have happened. Remember when Biron's cows tried to storm the town hall?"

Bip nodded in recollection. What had come to be known as the Great Bovine Rebellion had ended firstly in riots then mainly in steak.

In a community where people often tampered with the very fabric of nature, phenomena such as super-intelligent livestock were a commonplace occurrence.

"Thanks, Michaelmas. If they find out I'm practicing psyence without proper supervision, they'll have my guts for garters," said Bip.

"No problem, lad, but if yer going to practice, then…erm…do it elsewhere, would you? I don't need no more home improvements if you get my drift."

Bip nodded and ambled off, leaving Michaelmas to stare at what had formerly been his house.

CAPTAIN FINNEGUN REVIEWED his crew in an emergency assembly on the foredeck of the *Sentinel*. Everyone was present, still bleary-eyed from the abrupt ejection from chronostatic sleep. Looking out over the crowd of nearly identical gray and yellow uniforms, Finnegun cleared his throat.

"Ladies and gentlemen," he began, rather lamely. "It appears that we have been activated far before our estimated crisis intervention deadline by what appears to be an unexpected crisis of our very own."

The crew began to murmur until a man to Finnegun's left hushed them to quiet. Finnegun continued. "The situation is as follows—a large spherical metal object of unknown origin has struck the ship. While there is no major damage to life support or the primary structure of the ship, we have, I regret to say, been knocked out of orbit—"

A harassed looking woman in the crowd raised her voice. "So we're hurtling out into space, then?"

"Not quite, no. Not really," said Finnegun. The crew let out a collective sigh of relief. "We are, in fact, hurtling toward the planet's surface." He gestured to the giant holo-screen behind him, where the planet Bersch waited like a blue and green fist. The crew gazed at their fate with carefully blank expressions. The fact that they didn't begin shouting and screaming in a general panic said a lot about their nature.

The same harassed woman floored another question. "Shouldn't we just use the maneuvering thrusters, then?" There was a more positive murmur of agreement from the crew.

"Ah, good question that, good observation," said Finnegun. "But I'm afraid that's the problem you see; the actual aforementioned metal sphere is, in fact, lodged in our main engine, causing...let's say...a bit of a mess in the fuel ducts. Any attempt to utilize the maneuvering thrusters, or any other means of propulsion for that matter, could very well result in our being blown to smithereens."

Once again, Finnegun surveyed the rows of expectant faces. There were some times when being a captain wasn't an easy job. At the moment, he was hard pressed to think of a time when it had ever been easy.

A technician put his hand up to speak. "No disrespect, sir, but...erm...you are Elite-Gifted, sir. Couldn't you just...I dunno...convince the metal object it doesn't want to be lodged in the engine?" he finished, carefully probing the electric fence of fate, hoping to avoid a nasty shock.

Captain Finnegun smiled broadly. "Very good," he said. "Very good indeed—a superb suggestion. Alas, it wouldn't work. The problem being, you see, that if we by any means removed the sphere, it would leave a dirty great hole in the ship that might cause us all to implode."

The expressions of the crew turned slightly blanker. The technician spoke again. "Is there any chance we could repair it?"

Captain Finnegun clapped his hands together. "You really are a keen one, aren't you? Repair it? Yes, of course, and you chaps are just the sorts to do it, aren't you? With your tools and your mechanical ingenuity and whatnot. But I have to ask, to be on the safe side, how long would you think it would take?"

"Weeerrrlll..." began the technician, rolling his eyes toward the ceiling in a manner common to all mechanics across the ultraverse. "Repairing the main engine and a hull breach? If I got all the lads involved and worked straight through, we could get it repaired in say...seven hours? Five if you wanted a rush job."

Finnegun whistled through his teeth. "That's a damn pity, damn pity," he said. "Because, you see, we have less than two hours before we hit the planet's surface."

The harassed woman looked thoughtful for several seconds before flooring another question. "Well that's a bit of a bugger, isn't it?" she asked.

There was a general murmur of agreement.

2

Psyence, Hostility Advice and
Things that go Bang.

B ip sighed. It was a sigh that was comforting in its familiarity. It was sigh of resignation despite ambition. It was a sigh of the eternal soul who, for the millionth time, has pushed a boulder up a hill only to watch, for the millionth time, the boulder roll back down again. It was a well-tailored and expertly delivered sigh that would make anyone present feel the immediate desire to ask Bip what was wrong, then possibly make him a cup of tea. But Bip was alone, and here—in a rather pleasant meadow where sheep grazed and cows plotted revenge—there was no kettle in which to make tea.

Bip was thinking about employment. It was a perfectly natural thing to get depressed about for a seventeen-year-old in Kaneq, with his schooling years behind him and a lifelong career ahead of him. Come the apprentice fair, those of age would be taken aside by Kaneq's employers and ushered into trades most suited to their abilities and ambitions. As far as Bip was concerned, there was only one job that suited him. He wanted to be a psyentist.

All the children of Kaneq had psyentific potential from birth, a gift passed down from the near-mythic ancestors who had founded the community centuries ago. Those who showed more knack than others were encouraged to develop their talents throughout their education, and those of a significant enough talent were more often than not taken on as apprentices to the council, or more rarely employed to assist the elders. Kaneq had a tiny population, only a few thousand, so those who had significant talent were recognized very quickly. Bip had not been recognized. He sighed deeply again.

There were plenty of other jobs in Kaneq, but most of them required skills, patience, or a level of effort that Bip just wasn't cut out for. The trouble with the Kaneq way of life was that there were plenty of jobs essential to the running of the village, but if you wanted to get paid for doing very little, then the options were quite limited. Hard work and diligence were required by all to ensure the smooth running of the isolated settlement, and there was no room for laziness.

Sadly, Bip wasn't particularly keen on a life of good-natured diligence. No. With his scrawny frame and his aversion to hard work, Bip felt he was far better suited to working in an academic position. More specifically, the position of apprentice psyentist.

He had only ever heard about what it was the psyentists actually did with their time. The exclusive group was very secretive about their activities, spending all of their working life in the great, snow-covered, dome-shaped building at the very edge of the village known to the town folk simply as the dome. However, he had heard rumors that most of an apprentice's time was spent either studying the legendary archives or maintaining the heatshield that prevented the community from becoming a pointy pile of snow. Bip marveled. That kind of quiet life enriched with non-challenging work was more than he could ever hope for. And people thought the psyentists were dull!

He desperately wanted to be a psyentist, but he was filled with nagging doubt. He knew he had talent—even compared to some of the journeymen, his potential was remarkable. It was quite a difficult thing to turn an entire house and garden shed into an igloo. But his talent was unreliable, often disastrously so.

With fresh resolve, Bip decided to continue his practice. Rolling up the sleeves of his baggy gray jumper, he lay belly-down on the soft grass and focused on a hapless daisy that happened to be the nearest target. Squinting hard, Bip tried to convince the flower that it needed to grow to double its current size. It was quite simple to reach the flower's essence; sensing the common energies at its core was the easiest part of the process. Tears of concentration blurred his vision as he gently persuaded the flower to grow. A daisy was a hard target, far more complex than, say, a brick, but Bip needed to develop his skill to a level where it would not fail to impress the council come the apprentice fair.

Bip concentrated.

Concentrated…

As far as daisies go, this one was fairly blameless and did not deserve to be accidentally blown into tiny hay-feverish powder. Bip sat back, a petal hanging rather sadly from the end of his nose. He sighed. There was a lot of work to be done if he ever wanted to be a psyentist…

THE *SENTINEL* BEGAN its slow but deadly plummet toward the surface of Bersch. Inside, the harassed-looking woman took the floor. Her name was Izzy, and she was a junior technician. The gray boilersuit-like uniform did very little for a figure that would politely be called curvy but would more accurately be called dumpy. She was young and harbored an adolescent aggression that most people of the crew's culture had to be specially trained for. Currently, she was standing with her fists balled at her sides in futile anger.

"So what you're saying, Captain, is that with all of our most skilled technicians and all of you Elite-Gifted, we get blown out of orbit by a bit of space-rock?"

Finnegun rubbed his eyes. Every member of the crew was highly trained in various specialized fields, and for the last twenty minutes, they had been feverishly conducting thought experiments as to how they could escape the rather urgent predicament they found themselves in. So far it had all been to no avail, and usually with such a high concentration of genius, twenty minutes of intense thought was enough to provide at least a few solutions. The fact of the matter was that nobody on the ship could devise a way out of the current situation because nobody on the ship had ever thought it possible *to be* in this situation. He decided to turn to what the crew always felt was the last resort.

"Handen Strike?" he said. The man to Finnegun's left, who had been standing stock still during the hubbub, turned to look at his captain. "Handen, would you be so good as to take the floor?"

Handen nodded and cleared his throat. Instantly, the attention of the room focused upon him. Those who knew anything about the culture or home worlds of Finnegun and his crew would be surprised to see Handen amongst their registry. He was neither technician nor Elite-Gifted, but to the crew of the ship, he was something far rarer and, in some ways, far more important. He was a hostilities advisor.

Other cultures may have referred to Handen as a chief of security or defense secretary, but hostilities advisor was more like a combination of field marshal, general, man-at-arms, and security guard. Handen had a very important job for the sole reason that he was unique among his comrades in his knowledge about the concept of violence, weaponry, and other general products of hostility.

The crew of the *Sentinel* could not fathom that there were intelligent beings who might, for any reason, want to cause them harm. This was because the crew were Clarions—a completely peaceful race, and also because of their unique gifts and superb technological abilities, an extremely advanced one. Unfortunately, the major gap in their otherwise outstanding intellects was the ability to recognize when someone was eyeing them up for a fight.

Throughout the history of the Clarions, many embarrassing and disastrous events had occurred due to the simple fact that they could not recognize potential for hostility in a situation, let alone deal with it. People like Handen were a rare breed on the home worlds, fewer than one in a thousand of the total population. Any signs of aggression in a Clarion child meant careful nurturing for selective training. Having nothing like a standing army, the sole reason for the continuation of the Clarion culture is that the hostility advisors have always been present to tell the them what a gun is and how to build a much bigger one than their enemies have.

If not for men like Handen, the Clarions would have spent their time scratching their heads in confusion as space pirates made off with their houses.

Handen spoke. The crew listened. "Precisely forty minutes ago, the *Sentinel* was struck by an external, almost certainly man-made object, resulting in the disruption of our orbital trajectory and the disabling of our ability to maneuver in any way. Unfortunately for us, the object has penetrated the one part of the ship that its collective crew cannot repair in an appropriate time period—"

Izzy interrupted, "No offense, Handen, but we know all this already."

Handen retorted with a cool gaze. Izzy began to feel a touch uncomfortable under his deadpan stare. Handen continued. "After studying the estimated trajectory of the object and collating the available evidence, I have come to the conclusion that the object originated from the surface of Bersch and is the direct result of a hostile action."

The crew began to murmur in shock. Handen waited for them to try to comprehend what he had just said. A technician raised her hand to speak. "I'm not quite following you..."

Handen sighed and punched in a code sequence on a small console attached to his wrist. Behind him, the huge holographic display flickered and changed. It showed a picture of a cannon on a beach and a gaudily colored ship bobbing merrily on the ocean.

"Observe," said Handen.

The crew watched with delighted interest as the cannon made an exciting booming sound and flashed a pretty color, giving birth to a ball of some kind. Their delight quickly faded as the newborn spherical object crushed the gaudy ship into pieces. The presentation had effectively highlighted the gravity of the situation. It was weapons-grade hostility in a nutshell, really.

Handen spoke while he still had the crew's horrified attention. "It appears we have underestimated the evolution of the people of Bersch. It appears they are at the stage of technological advancement where they can pinpoint the engine block of an orbital target with a ballast-style weapon. Unfortunately for us, it seems they have not yet evolved to the point where they can ask questions first."

Finnegun had been looking thoughtful throughout Handen's demonstration. "Surely, even if we have underestimated their rate of advancement that much, they are nowhere near a level of technology that would allow them to penetrate our shields?" he said.

Handen nodded. "I've consulted the Mother Tongue, and it's not picking up any readable signals, not even radio. With this in mind, it's probably safe to assume that the people of Bersch have nothing within their arsenal sophisticated enough to penetrate our shields, Captain," he said. "However, when the Sentinel is in its sleeper cycle, it drops and reconfigures its primary repellent field every seventy-two hours. I'm not sure if the people of Bersch are aware of this weakness, but the evidence is too grave to suggest coincidence. My opinion stands that we are victims of a well-formulated and malicious hostile attack from the planet's surface."

The crew gasped. Izzy looked as though she would burst into tears of frustration.

"But...why? Why would someone want to blow up that pretty ship? Let alone us?"

Again, Handen sighed, then took a sheet of paper from his notepad, screwed it into a ball, and launched it at Izzy's forehead. It made a satisfactory smacking sound. Izzy's eyes went wide in shock and fear.

"Why did you do that?"

"Because I can," replied Handen. It was the most basic demonstration of why hostility existed and what the consequences were, but Handen had found himself repeating it countless times during his service to the *Sentinel*. It was an example that tended to get the message across, if only for a short time.

Finnegun, who had also been staring in horror at Handen's destructive capabilities, shook himself and returned his focus to the matter at hand. "Do you suspect pan-dimensional influence?" he asked.

Handen thought for a moment. "The attack has all the hallmarks of adverse randominity, sir, but there are no readings to suggest any recent dimensional transgressions."

Finnegun frowned. "Hmm. Not the Discordance, then." He looked up, focusing his attention on the hostilities advisor. "What do you suggest we do, Handen?"

"With respect, Captain, retaliation would be futile. A waste of power. I suggest we use the Mother Tongue to send a message back to command central explaining our situation and then..." He swept the crew with his stony stare. "Then we prepare ourselves for a crash landing."

IT MIGHT or might not have pleased Handen to know that the large ball of metal lodged in his ship had been put there entirely by accident. It so happened that down on the planet's surface, Lord Draegul III—ruler of the Argustin Empire, supreme commander of the world's most feared and powerful army—was a bit of an enthusiast when it came to things that went *bang*. Indeed, it was this enthusiasm, shared by his father and grandfather before him, that had led to many of the military and territorial advancements of the Empire. Draegul's army possessed the most finely crafted swords as well as the sturdiest armor and a nightmarish array of siege weaponry, most of which was of his own innovation. It was one of these monstrous contraptions that currently commanded his attention.

The Research in Death Development Master stood nervously ringing his hands. The weapon known as the Giant's Middle Finger was technically of his devising. Draegul himself had commissioned it, requesting a weapon that with one shot could lay waste to a small castle as well as rudely offend his enemies. The Master had exceeded his own expectations and taken his knowledge of trajectory and dynamics to new levels in order to create what was, essentially, a really big trebuchet with a suggestively stylized launching arm.

Draegul had been pleased with the results and had spent a few wars merrily crushing (and offending) small villages and hamlets alike, but—as with most new toys—Draegul had soon grown bored with it and demanded a weapon that could lay waste to an entire *city* in one shot. The Research Master had spent many months pleading with Lord Draegul to reconsider—the Giant's Middle Finger (Mark 1) was already extremely dangerous to the operators as well as the victims, and anything of a greater scale was likely to be disastrous. But Lord Draegul had insisted, and there was nothing like Lord Draegul's insistence—which was usually coupled with the promise of agony—to focus the mind.

It had taken five years and enough gold to feed several small countries and had cost the lives of countless engineers and apprentices, but finally the Giant's Middle Finger (Mark 2) was locked, loaded, and pointed at the only safe target available—the sky.

Draegul bounced on his heels in anticipation, his dark features taken over by an eerily pleasant smile. He surveyed his new toy from the high tower of his palace—and "surveyed" was the word, as the weapon was over ten times the size of the original Mark 1 device. It was stood far outside the capital city's walls, lit against the night by countless torches and bonfires. Its wheels were blocked and bolstered with stone constructions the size of large houses. You could hear the strain and scream of miles of rope and pulley as it struggled against its payload—a gargantuan ball of pure iron the size of an uberbeast.

The Research Master had wisely made himself scarce. He knew all too well that the pent-up force of the monstrous weapon was unlikely to be purely directed at the sky. He had several nasty suspicions about the feasibility of the GMF's structural ability to withstand its own force, all of which he had voiced to Lord Draegul and all to no avail.

Draegul gazed up to the stars from beneath the long, thin fringes of his raven-colored hair. The stars had always annoyed him slightly, and although the night sky was merely a testing ground for his new weapon, he secretly hoped he might knock down a few of them, just to teach them a lesson.

"One day," Draegul whispered under his breath, "I'll rule everything I see. Including those glittering bastards." As he spoke, he began to hear echoes of encouraging whispers at the back of his mind…

He was brought back from his megalomaniacal musings by the discreet throat-clearing of a royal aide. He shook his head and tried to remember where he was and what he was doing. Ah, yes—he was on the palace balcony, preparing to address his subjects, who were gathered in the city's capital square, shuffling their feet and glancing around with a growing sense of unease. Draegul clapped his hands twice, indicating that he was prepared to begin his ceremonial address. He needn't have bothered with the gesture; the assembled crowd was already listening politely and attentively. This was mainly because anyone who didn't listen politely and attentively was promptly taken away and beaten by attentive yet extremely impolite royal guardsmen.

"My loyal subjects," shouted Draegul, his reedy voice amplified by a huge cone of metal. "Today we witness yet another triumph in the glorious reign of the Draegul succession." He raised his arms to the sky and basked in the nervous pattering of applause of the crowd below. "It is with great pride that I, Tragus Thomas Tomberry Draegul the Third, unveil a weapon fit to poke the eye of God, a weapon huge enough to compensate for my crippling emotional inadequacies, a weapon of such magnitude and horror that I probably shouldn't even use it…"

The crowd held their collective breath at the small glimmer of hope Draegul's sudden moment of sanity had presented.

"But I'm going to anyway," he finished, and the crowd chided themselves for their foolish optimism.

Draegul continued. "It is but one more rung in the golden ladder that is the immortality of the Draegul succession. May the Lord bless me and keep me. And some of the people I like as well. But not all of them." Lord Draegul sat back and enjoyed yet more nervous applause, and even some impromptu cheering from those members of the crowd closest to the watchful glare of the royal guardsmen.

Feeling happier than he had since he'd first pulled the legs from an insect, Lord Draegul lifted a silken handkerchief above his head, giving the signal to fire. The secondary watchtower received the signal and relayed it to the next watchtower, which, in turn, gave the order to fire to the trigger operator. Without hesitation the operator, picked solely for his idiocy, took his torch and set fire to the GMF's trigger rope. It was to the credit of the Research Master's genius that several thousand tons of tension caused by the deadly contraption was held back by a stretch of entwined rope no more than a meter thick.

There were a few minutes of suspicious quiet as the GMF's trigger rope began to burn. Some of the more realistically minded of the research and engineering team ran very quickly in various directions.

Without warning, the trigger rope snapped like the sound of a god smacking his forehead in frustration. There was a flurry of confused whipping sounds as a chain reaction of releasing ropes happened in a split of a second. A deep rumble began almost instantaneously.

Lord Draegul fought hard to keep the expression of manic glee from his face as the rumbling reached a thunderous crescendo. There was a sonic boom as the GMF's launching finger was released, flipping the bird to the entire world. No sooner had it done so than, succumbing to the massive conflicting forces of kinetic energy and friction, the entirety of the Giant's Middle Finger exploded with an earth-shattering bang and a cracking flash of brilliant white. Countless pieces of flaming shrapnel no larger than toothpicks zipped lethally for miles around, burning, impaling, and obliterating anything with the misfortune to get in the way. An almighty cloud of red-hot dust shot into the air and rolled slowly and menacingly toward the city, much to the horror of its occupants. The larger pieces of shrapnel that had launched at unimaginable speeds into the skies above began to pelt haphazardly into the ground, causing massive craters wherever they descended. Lord Draegul was oblivious to the apocalyptic destruction around him; the screams and thunder of his burning city proved no distraction to him. He was watching, with an expression of awful ecstasy, the glowing arc of the ballast's pure iron tip, successfully launched and burning a painfully bright white as it rocketed toward the stars like an angel who has just remembered he's left the kettle on. He wiped a tear from his eye as the ballistic ballast winked into nothingness, spanning a distance too far for him to follow. Then he laughed maniacally, as mad people are want to do in such situations.

Various cultures across the globe of Bersch looked up in awe at the reverse shooting star, and a lot of excited astronomers made a lot of inaccurate assumptions. Not by one was it predicted that the object was a rogue metal sphere that would spell doom for the *Sentinel* and the sleeping alien species that watched over them. In fact, the only accurate reading of the celestial anomaly was by a poorly educated astronomer called Harry Fudeperred who was rumored to have observed the gleaming arc and exclaimed, "Crap. This can't be good."

3

Tuesday is a Good Day to Die

Captain Finnegun adjusted his seat harness for what seemed like the hundredth time. Clarions were by nature a very calm and thoughtful people, but Finnegun couldn't help but be slightly unnerved by the prospect of an entire planet punching him in the face.

He looked about him. The ship's intellium hull had flawlessly transmuted into an arrowhead shape, all the better to combat the sudden turbulence of entering Bersch's atmosphere. Almost the entirety of the crew was assembled near the center of the arrow, strapped in tightly to their seats and focusing all their energies on maintaining the aerodynamic new shape of the *Sentinel*. Two engineers and an Elite-Gifted had volunteered to stay in the engine rooms in an attempt to divert shield and engine power to where it would count in free-fall. The plan was that as soon as they had escaped the lethal vacuum of space, they would remove the metal sphere from the engine block and see if the ship's descent could be slowed by one last burst of the maneuvering thrusters before the engine fell to pieces. Finnegun grimly suspected that the engine would explode before any of the thrusters could be utilized. He admired the bravery of the volunteers but couldn't help but regret that their sacrifice might ultimately be for naught. The *Sentinel* was never designed to plummet unpowered through the air.

He looked at Handen, who was seated to his left. The big man didn't take his eyes from the view screen, where the steadily expanding bulk of Bersch loomed menacingly.

"Twenty seconds until we enter the atmosphere, Captain," he stated matter-of-factly.

"Wonderful," muttered the captain. "And how is our angle of descent?"

"Not great," replied Handen, scanning over the rapidly scrolling charts of information on the holographic side monitor. "I think we can expect a bit of turbulence, actually. Ten seconds."

Finnegun sighed. In ten seconds, it appeared life was going to be terminally interesting. He spared a few moments contemplation for the message he had sent via light wave to the Clarion home system. The message had calmly detailed the *Sentinel's* dilemma and Finnegun's recommended course of action, along with a few messages from crew members who had used what might be the last moments of their existence to put their affairs in order. Captain Finnegun was a tad worried. He had sent the distress message via the most logical and efficient system of wormholes he could calculate, but even with his precise calculations, he wondered if his people would be in time to save the world. In the large stretch of infinity that stood between Bersch and the Clarion systems, there was a lot that could go wrong.

He looked around at the crew again. A few of them had tightly shut their eyes or were muttering rapidly under their breath. Finnegun had never been one for unnecessary drama, but now, with the prospect of total destruction rocketing toward them, he decided it might be time for a few heroic last words.

"What day is it?" he asked Handen, who looked briefly puzzled before answering.

"Tuesday."

"Ah," said Finnegun. "I suppose that's as good a day as any to die..."

And with that, the *Sentinel* entered the atmosphere of Bersch.

BIP GLANCED AROUND NERVOUSLY. The hubbub of the apprentice fair had always been a pleasant diversion when he was younger, but now, standing on a wooden platform with the other young men and women for the entire community to gawk at, Bip felt uneasy.

The people of Kaneq treated the apprentice fair as a holiday. Traditionally it lasted for four days, two for the choosing and allocation of apprentices, one day purely for a celebration of their new starts in life, and a final day to nurse the inevitable hangover. Becoming an apprentice was very much a coming-of-age ceremony for the youth of Kaneq.

The crowd mulled around the marketplace, which was far more active than usual, providing a brisk trade in cold beer and candied treats. The psyentists had taken extra care to ensure the filtered weather would be clement for the day. A warm, gentle breeze was textured with merry music from the various bards and bands, while bunting hung in the air, swaying as though dancing. An atmosphere of merriment and a tang of excitement made for a happy crowd, while the warm smells of roasting chestnuts and tart cider honeyed the air.

Bip looked around at the other potential apprentices. Many of them wore expressions of cocky self-assuredness, others looked vaguely anxious, and only one or two looked as petrified as Bip felt. A long, drawn-out yawn caught Bip's attention and he turned and looked into a familiar face. The face, green-hued and waxy, belonged to Bailey, an old classmate of Bip's who wanted nothing more than to apprentice in the fields of hospitality and distillery. The burly lad looked into Bip's eyes and belched quietly.

"I feel sick," he said.

"What's up with you?" said Bip with a frown. "Surely you can't be worried? You've spent your entire education learning about beer and beer-related activities."

"I'm not worried," muttered the larger youth, flicking his greasy fringe away from his eyes and pinching the bridge of his nose. "It's just that I've got a stinking hangover. Bit of last minute primary research the other day…and night…"

Bip sighed. *You have to admire such dedication to one's calling*, he thought.

A sudden trumpet blare announced the beginning of the ceremony, causing Bip to stumble and nearly fall from the podium. He turned his attention to the gaudily decorated stage of address, where the senior councilmen and various craft masters began to fill the vacant seats. When everyone had been seated, a second trumpet blare announced the arrival of the elders.

They filed in slowly and crookedly, uniformly ancient and hunched under their dark black robes of office and their flat-brimmed hats. On cursory examination, it was difficult to see the purpose the revered elders held in the community of Kaneq. They were generally referred to as the Keepers of the Ancient Wisdom, although what this ancient wisdom was, no one was entirely sure. Even so, the elders held a prominent place at all meetings and events of importance.

After what seemed like an age they were seated, and finally, with one last trumpet blare, Truggle, eldest of the elders, began his slow progress to the center of the stadium. He was far older-looking than the other elders, with a long, crooked nose and long, crooked beard that fought for dominance under his tufty-bald head.

He did not walk anywhere these days, his frail form instead supported by a chair modified with swiveling wheels on each leg. He steered and propelled the chair with an old broom, and this, coupled with the fact that the hem of Truggle's ceremonial robes obscured most of the wheeled chair, made him appear to be an ancient, gliding janitor.

The crowd hushed as Truggle prepared to give his traditional opening speech, which would signify the official beginning of the choosing. With a sound like a cat choking on a fishbone, he cleared his throat.

"Ladies and Gentlemen. Bloody hell, is it that time of year again? You know, it doesn't seem that long ago that I was down there with you lot, wondering what I'd be. And now, here am I, being what I would be regardless. Makes you wonder if there's any point in worrying about anything at all, seeing as things sort of just happen whether you like it or not. On the other hand, it's not as if you can just lie around in bed all day and hope for the best, can you? Or can you? Well, you can if you like, I suppose, I'm not your mum. Anyway..."

There was a long pause as Truggle sat in contemplative silence. Eventually he began to snore, and a kindly councilman wheeled the elder away from the stage. The assembled crowd began to applaud politely, this being one of the most coherent speeches Truggle had given in a long time.

Dunman, the chief councilman and closest thing Kaneq had to a leader, took the center of the Stadium of Address. He polished his small, round spectacles with a handkerchief and smoothed down his unnaturally smooth hair before he spoke in his awkward and wobbly voice.

"Ladies and Gentlemen, today we make futures not just for the individual, but for the community."

"The community," chorused the crowd, the line finely rehearsed over countless public events.

"You may begin," announced Dunman, and the crowd once again boiled into a busy throng. Immediately Bip spotted the senior psyentists who would likely be doing the choosing. Their long white robes and high collars stood out clearly in the surging crowd. As they began to approach the large podiums where the potentials waited, Bip puffed out his chest and smiled broadly.

"Cut that out," muttered Bailey. "You look like a nutter."

Bip sagged back into a more natural stance, looking as deflated as he felt. Suddenly, Bailey seemed to stiffen as a figure bustled through the crowd toward them. It was Michaelmas. With a flurry that was the closest the morose youth had ever reached to urgency, Bailey began to rake the hair out of his face and blink the sleep out of his eyes.

"Oi," he whispered to Bip. "It's the landlord from the Empty Goat!"

"What, you mean Michaelmas?" said Bip, perversely pleased by being on a first-name basis with one of Bailey's potential employers.

"You know him?" gasped the hungover hopeful. "Could you put in a good word?"

"I'll see what I can do," said Bip smugly (although he doubted how much he could sway the opinion of someone, friend or not, whose house he had turned into an igloo).

"Mornin', Bip," Michaelmas hailed him as he approached the boys. "You'll be pleased to know that the council have returned my house to normal and are keeping a sharp eye out for the vandals concerned." Michaelmas gave Bip a non-too-subtle wink before turning his attention to Bailey, who did his best to stand up straight without swaying from side to side.

"Now then, young Bailey." The rough-looking lad's eyes widened at being recognized. "Yeah tha's right, I've been keeping an eye on you, lad." Michaelmas grinned. "They tell me yer quite the expert on bar studies?"

Bailey tried to formulate an intelligent reply but only succeeded in making a modest grunting noise.

Michaelmas clapped the tall youth on the shoulder. "Come on then, my lad, you and I has lots to talk about!"

The two alcohol enthusiasts walked out into the crowd talking about the intricacies of both the consumption and brewing of fine booze. Bip watched them go with rising sadness. Bip, like many people on the right side of the bar, assumed that beer was beer and that was all there was to it. To hear Michaelmas and Bailey drivel on about matters of physics and biology seemed a touch absurd. Beer, he had always thought, went in one way and out of the other, taking a bit of your common sense with it. That there was expert logic and research behind the process seemed ludicrous. However, what really annoyed Bip was that, as silly as the whole affair seemed, Bailey looked likely to gain a life career in something he loved, while Bip was left standing on the podium in an ever-decreasing gaggle of youths.

His heart sank as he saw the senior psyentists pull a young girl from the crowd and walk off, chatting excitedly, not even glancing in his direction.

THE EMPTY GOAT thudded and vibrated to the beat of an energetic folk band. The air hung heavy with sweet smoke and the musky atmosphere of many people crowded into a relatively small space. Although the celebrations weren't supposed to begin until the following night, many of the potentials who had been chosen on the first day were starting early.

The center of the Empty Goat, normally filled with tables and chairs, had been cleared to make a serviceable dance floor in front of a stage made up of beer crates and planks. The band was playing a stomping beat, and the dancers whirled with no signs of slowing down. Amongst the merry-makers, well-wishers, and good-natured drunks, one face stood out as being terminally depressed. Bip sat in a darkened corner drinking from a tankard larger than his head.

Bailey and Michaelmas had taken the night off to "welcome Bailey to the family" and were getting roaring drunk on some of the Empty Goat's finer celebration ales. They shouted at one another in the manner of those too inebriated to realize they were shouting as they manhandled another barrel of beer from Michaelmas's personal collection over to Bip's table.

Bip was vaguely aware he had drunk far too much but was much too upset to care. He hadn't been picked. While various potentials were taken aside as willing apprentices to willing masters, Bip had been left standing like an idiot, the last on his podium, until Dunman had signaled the end of the first day of choosing. Despite Bip's initial urge to crawl into bed and cry, Bailey had persuaded him to join in the premature celebrations with the vain promise of finding solace at the bottom of a tankard. So far, all Bip had found at the bottom of the tankard was the reflection of his miserable face, and the desire to get another tankard.

"Cheer up!" yelled Bailey with annoying enthusiasm. "Anyone would think you hadn't been picked or something!"

"Well, I haven't, actually," said Bip, reproachfully.

"Oh...yeah...well, what I mean is...I mean to say..." Bailey looked confused for a moment. "I do beg your pardon, I appear to have lost all ability to articulate a cogent retort," he said, and turned his attention back to his beer.

"What he means," Michaelmas interjected, "is that there's still a whole other day of choosing left. Not everybody gets picked on the first day. It'll be all right!"

"But what if I don't get picked on the second day?" said Bip.

Michaelmas knitted his brow in concentration for a while. "Come to think of it," he said eventually, "I don't think that's ever happened."

"Then what if I'm the first?" Bip wailed. "I'll be a laughing stock!"

"Now, now, Bip," Michaelmas said, patting him reassuringly on the shoulder. "Even if you don'ts get picked—and that's a big *if*, mind you—the community'll take care of you."

"What, like some kind of charity case? I don't see how that's supposed to make me feel better. Even Derren Doonby got picked as an apprentice lumberjack, and he's much less qualified than I am!"

"Oi!" said Bailey, looking up from his tankard. "I won't hear a bad word said about Derren—he knows more about wood and trees than anyone I know, and I'm sure he'll make a great lumberjack!"

"But he's got no hands!" said Bip. "How is he supposed to hold an axe?"

"All right there, Bip, I knows yer upset, but bad-mouthing young Derren won't help anyone," scolded Michaelmas.

"Sorry," mumbled Bip. "I'm just...sorry."

"Look, I'll tell you what," said Michaelmas leaning over conspiratorially. "If the worst comes to the worst and nobody picks you, you could always come and work for me as a kitchen boy. I know it ain't much, but you could apprentice here for a few years while you practice your psyence, and then maybe you could reapply for another apprenticeship later on down the road."

"You'd do that? I mean, I know you've already more staff than you need," Bip said.

"Not a problem, me ol'mate. Yer pappy would have wanted it." Michaelmas sniffed and rubbed an emerging tear from his eye.

Bip shifted uncomfortably. When Michaelmas was drunk, he

would often talk about Bip's father, who had left Kaneq thirteen years ago and never returned. Bip had never really known the man but was assured by his mother and the various village-folk that *had* known him that he was a great man with commendable psyentific talent.

"Great man, was your pappy," mumbled Michaelmas, gazing dreamy-eyed into a happy memory. "Did I ever tell you about the time when—"

"I'm sure you did, Michaelmas," Bip interrupted. "But I don't mind hearing it again."

CAPTAIN FINNEGUN OPENED his eyes again and, with a great deal of effort, managed to unclench his teeth. He looked over at Handen, who was still grimacing at the view screen. He turned to the screen himself and gasped.

A few minutes ago, but which had seemed like hours, they had entered Bersch's atmosphere, experiencing not so much turbulence as an extremely localized hurricane. While the *Sentinel* had been beaten about quite badly on its entry, the inner environmental functions had remained stable, meaning that the crew had been neither burnt to a crisp nor pressurized to the point of implosion.

Instead, they experienced an uneasy feeling of weightlessness as the ship fell toward Bersch at a faster rate than the gravity stabilizers could compensate for. The clouds had cleared from the view screen to reveal an endless blue void looming ominously below them as they headed toward one of Bersch's larger oceans. Finnegun, who had not seen any geographic detail first hand in several millennia, could not help but feel awed.

Handen checked their angle of descent. The modified shape of the *Sentinel* was dealing with the aerodynamics surprisingly well; they were falling rapidly but maintaining a sound forward trajectory. He quickly checked the short-range scanners for the nearest landmass.

"Captain," he said, "I've got a suitable landing site for us coming up. Virtually uninhabited, plenty of flat space, a few mountains, but—"

Finnegun interrupted. "Are there any alternative landing sites? Excluding the bottom of the sea, I mean."

"Well…" said Handen, checking the scanner screen. "No."

"Well, then, it seems that the decision of where to crash has been made for us. Engage manual controls."

Handen complied and pressed a short sequence of buttons on a nearby keypad. Outside, various flaps and shoots unbuckled from the flawless silver skin of the starship. In the cockpit, a joystick emerged in front of the captain's chair.

"Mr. Strike," Finnegun said. "I understand that as a hostilities advisor you are a man of some experience when it comes to quick reactions and so on?"

"Yes, sir."

"I wonder if you'd do us the honor of piloting the craft and attempting to avoid our seemingly inevitable destruction?"

"Yes, sir." Handen pressed another sequence of keys and the joystick retracted and reappeared in front of his seat. A targeting monitor showing the distance to the landing site and the ship's altitude and speed of descent closed over one of his eyes. The main view screen began to depict the landscape in a series of green and blue lines with various measurements and probability lines drawn here and there in red.

Finnegun turned back to the crew and watched their calm faces as they engaged in the various tasks assigned to them. As Handen began his attempt to glide the craft, the sound of rushing air began to permeate the hull. Finnegun thought briefly how eerie the sound was in the dead silence of the foredeck.

4

Rejection, Penguins and the Truth about Everything

Bip tried to fight the feeling of overwhelming embarrassment that crawled over him like an army of spiders. It was quite difficult. He was once more on the podium with the other potentials, surrounded by the gawking crowds. The main difference was that this time, instead of being surrounded by comfortable numbers of people in the same situation, there were only three potentials left. Including him.

The second day of choosing had been an unglamorous affair, with the remaining potentials being plucked from the crop quickly and quietly while Bip stood feeling as stupid as he thought he looked. Not one psyentist had approached him. In fact, he hadn't even *seen* a psyentist all day.

Bip looked at his two companions on the podium. All that remained of the good and great had been selected early in the second day, and now Bip was left with "Half-Brick" Thompson and "Bogey" Betty Bogeyton. Bogey was a bright enough girl but had a rather disturbing odor of very old cabbage, which would saturate the senses if you spent too long around her. Half-Brick, however, was widely believed to be several baskets short of a picnic and had earned his nickname for famously being outwitted in a game of skill by half a brick. How this was actually possible no one knew, but the brick had won nevertheless. It wasn't long before a master tanner, whose sense of smell had long since given up, took Bogey aside for a new career. Bip was left standing with Half-Brick.

"I wants to be a farmer," said Half-Brick.

"Really," said Bip, expressing not one iota of interest.

"I wants to be a farmer and chase the penguins."

"That's good," said Bip. It was an essential job for an apprentice to chase the domesticated penguins of Kaneq, who were very extremely docile by nature and tended not to move around very much. If the penguins weren't chased sufficiently, they would become too fat and would be unable to move at all. And so the position of Penguin Chaser, while far from being dignified, at least warranted respect due to its necessity.

"I wants to shave the cows 'n all," added Half-Brick.

"That's good," said Bip. Shaving the domesticated Kaneqian snowcow of its ever-growing woolen coat was also an important job for an apprentice, providing materials for the looms and weavers and preventing the cows from becoming entangled in a giant ball of fluff.

Even Half-Brick, thought Bip, *who is clearly a danger to himself and those around him, is still more useful than me.* He sighed.

"I'd quite likes to be a cow," said Half-Brick.

"That's good," Bip said, and briefly contemplated a life of chasing penguins and shaving cows.

AT THE BACK of the crowd, two figures watched Bip from the shadows. One of them was hunched in a chair and smoked a long, rank pipe. The other wrung his hands and nervously smoothed his already smooth hair.

"I just don't see why we have to humiliate him like this."

"Leave him be," said the pipe smoker. "No point in giving him an apprenticeship. Not where he's going."

"Are you sure he's the right candidate? I mean, in a couple of years, he might make a good apprentice psyentist, but it seems unwise…"

"Don't you tell me what's unwise, my boy," hawked the figure through clouds of smoke. "I still remember you when you was knee-high to a penguin, and I was pretty damn wise back then too!"

"Sorry, Truggle, I forget myself. Just nerves, I suppose."

"That's all right, Dunman. These are nervous days…"

———

THE FARM MASTER circled Half-Brick and prodded him occasionally. He lifted the boy's lips to check his teeth and gave him a few more experimental prods before tipping back his flat cap of office and staring hard into Half-Brick's vacant eyes. Half-Brick stood rigidly, his face a picture of oblivion.

"I wonders if you can tell me, lad," said the farm master, "where you are at the moment?"

Half-Brick's face twisted into a rictus of concentration. "I'm ere, aren't I?" he concluded.

"Well, that's good enough for me," said the farm master. "Welcome aboard, my lad."

"What?" said Half-Brick, as he was led away to his new life.

Bip felt sick. He stood alone on the podium as the crowd began to dissipate. Suddenly a trumpet sounded, and Dunman waved to the crowd from the stadium of address.

"Thus we signal the end of the choosing," he said. "Let the celebrations begin!" There was a loud cheer from the crowd and a band began to play.

"Wait!" said Bip.

The crowd continued oblivious, gearing up for a celebration that would likely last all through the night and most of the following day.

"What about me?" wailed Bip. He searched desperately for Michaelmas in the crowd and finally located him at the back of the hubbub, where he was walking hurriedly away. "Michaelmas! Wait!" shouted Bip. Michaelmas lowered his head and continued to scutter away, clearly pretending not to have heard his friend. Tears of frustration began to well up in Bip's eyes and he balled his fists in the air. "Everybody wait!" he screamed, causing many people in the crowd to turn and watch the luckless potential with interest. He more or less had their complete attention.

It was his last resort, a trick he had been saving for a worst-case scenario such as this. A trick that couldn't fail to attract the attention of the psyentists. He concentrated all his will into bonding with the energies within the podium he stood upon and, with streams of sweat gliding down his face, persuaded the podium to rise into the air.

The theory of the process was relatively simple and was designed for showmanship rather than real effect. It was impossible to make the podium rise without making it lighter than air, therefore becoming a gas rather than a solid, and therefore no longer being a podium in the classic and relevant sense. Bip's trick was much simpler than levitation. He would convince the podium to redistribute its mass to its own center. The effect, Bip had planned, would be that as the podium grew smaller in its radius, the center (the part he was standing on) would be pushed into the air. Bip had been proud of the idea, and if it worked without a hitch, there would be no way for people to doubt his knack for psyence.

He concentrated hard...

Concentrated...

With a giant *whoosh* and a blinding flash that no one had been expecting, Bip's shoes caught fire. He blinked through his half-moon glasses in stupefied disbelief as he watched his burning shoes, then in a moment of horrified realization began a frenzied tap dance of panic. A lot of the crowd rushed to his aid, attempting to douse the flames with bottles and glasses of whatever they had been drinking. A lot of the crowd were too busy trying not to laugh. A lot more of the crowd couldn't help themselves and were laughing and hooting hysterically as Bip danced a crazed jig across the podium.

"What a thicko," said Half-Brick, shaking his head.

THE *SENTINEL* SOARED across an icy landscape, emitting a low roar as it inched closer and closer to impact.

Captain Finnegun watched the view screen with a growing sense of dread. In an attempt to kill some of the *Sentinel's* lethal speed, Handen had decelerated too much. Although they had safely reached the icy continent, they were a good hundred meters under their ideal angle of descent, and it looked likely they would catch the belly of the craft on a ragged pair of mountains before they reached their intended landing site. The only options were to attempt to decelerate more and risk a full-on collision with the mountains, or to find some way to regain the height they had lost. Finnegun watched a rearview monitor for a while, then calmly activated an intercom panel on his wrist.

"Officer Kanick," he said, "I wonder if perhaps this is the time for that little plan of yours?"

When the *Sentinel's* shape had been modified, the crew had moved the entire engine room, complete with breach, to the back end of the ship. Shortly before entering the atmosphere of Bersch, three of the crew had donned environment suits and redirected the repellent field to seal the rest of the ship off from the engine room. After doing this, they had harnessed their suits to the ship and safely dislodged the metal ballast from the hull, depressurizing the engine room and enabling them to begin repairs on the ravaged engine block. The intellium that served as the hull of the ship had begun to knit the breach into repair as soon as the obstruction had been removed, but the engine block and wiring were composed entirely of more common and stable materials, and they hadn't been able to make much progress in mending it. For the last few minutes, they had been grimly watching endless fields of ice rush beneath them through the slowly decreasing breach. The ground was beginning to look uncomfortably close.

Officer Kanick listened to his intercom. "Will do, Captain," he said, then turned to the engineers. "Well, chaps, looks like its plan B after all. Robinna, you ready the fuel flow. Christian, get ready with the warm-up ignition pistons."

The two engineers nodded.

"Wait for my mark," said Kanick, and looked at his wrist piece where a steady countdown marked their approaching doom. "I'd just like to say, chaps, all formalities aside, that it's been a damn pleasure working with you."

Robinna nodded, her flyaway blond hair clearly visible through her environment suit's domed helmet. "You too, Kanick," she said.

"Cheers, mate," said Christian, trying hard not to let his voice crack.

"Okay," said Kanick, with forced calm in his voice. "Fuel flow, go."

Robinna punched in a code sequence at a console, and various pieces of machinery began to whirr into life. At the hull breach, a severed tangle of pipes began to emit a clear gas with a loud *hussssss*.

"Warm-up ignition pistons, go," said Kanick. Christian hesitated for a moment, then punched in a code at his console. At the hull breach, a ton of obliterated wiring began to spark and smoke dangerously.

"I hope this works," said Kanick. And then his world went white.

Back on the foredeck, Finnegun clenched his fists as the mountains crawled quickly across the view screen. Impact was inevitable. Finnegun desperately tried to think of a course of action that, in the milliseconds available, might avoid the certainly fatal collision. Suddenly, a huge blast emitted from behind the vessel. Finnegun looked into the view screen with horror as the mountains flip-flopped upside down.

The explosion of the *Sentinel's* engine block as the leaking hyperfuel ignited had been titanic in its power, instantly snuffing out the lives of Kanick, Robinna, and Christian. It was only because of the redirected repellent field that the entire ship was not destroyed. Instead, the mighty blast acted as a boost to the falling craft, sending it spinning slightly upward.

Finnegun, despite developing nausea, managed to keep his eyes on the view screen. The mountains were still upside down, but rather than being directly in front of them, they now appeared to be directly above them. As the craft span around to its upright position it was, of course, revealed that the mountains were directly below them. The plan had worked. They had avoided collision with the mountains.

"Thank you, Kanick," whispered the captain, as he watched the trail of flaming debris in the rearview monitor.

BIP SAT ALONE in the graveyard, listening to the slow tweet of some nameless songbird. He didn't view the graveyard with any sort of romantic morbidity; it was just that here amongst Kaneq's dead and gone he would be able to avoid the rest of the village.

His father was buried around here somewhere, he knew. At least, *technically* his father had been buried here, though his actual body had never been recovered. It was an assumed grave for an assumed death, taking the view that anybody who had been missing in the Ice Plains for as long as Bip's father was either dead or...well, they were most likely dead.

Bip tried to imagine what his father might say to him now, if he were alive, tried to imagine what words of advice he might have for his unemployable son. It was difficult. He had never really been old enough to understand the man, who had been just another friendly face in the sky who'd picked him up when he was upset and kissed his forehead at bedtime. He realized with some dismay that he couldn't even conjure up what his father had sounded like.

He sat on a tombstone and stared glumly at Old Bachalack and the Patient Mother, the two mountains that permanently framed Kaneq's skyline. They were unchanging and familiar and extremely definite, and for this reason, they were normally a comforting sight for Bip in times of uncertainty. Not today, though. Today he sat lost in thoughts of a bleak future.

He was shaken from his reverie by the sudden crack of a snapping twig behind him.

"It's a bugger, isn't it? Death, I mean," Truggle said, rowing his rickety wheeled chair up to Bip's side, his peanut-like head dappled with sunlight.

Bip was surprised. Though he had been around Truggle before, this was as lucid as he had ever seen the elder. "I'm not thinking about death," he replied.

"Bloody hell, I am," said Truggle. "You start to, you know, when you get to my age."

Bip's curiosity overtook his etiquette. "How old are you, exactly?"

Truggle counted on his fingers. "About…about a hundred and sixty?" he ventured. "You don't pay as much attention to your age when you hit triple digits."

"A hundred and sixty? That's…well, that's very…old," Bip finished lamely.

"Thanks very much," said Truggle, cheerfully. "I intend to live for a good few years yet, though, so don't look at me like I'm half dust already." He chuckled for a moment, then leaned over toward Bip with a conspiratorial air. "They think I'm senile, you know," he whispered. "A few toys lost in the attic. But then, what do they know, eh? Best to let them think I'm barmy—saves me having to listen to them, at least."

"You mean you pretend to be mad?" Bip said, shocked despite his melancholy.

"I'm a wise old fool," Truggle mumbled, a distracted smile playing across his withered lips. "And what they don't know can't hurt them."

"I think that's utterly immoral," said Bip.

"I think it's bloody brilliant. You hear things, you know, when people think you're barmy. You learn a lot about people."

Bip stared at the ground, trying to indicate politely that he didn't wish to talk any further. A few minutes passed. In the silence, the sound of distant music could be heard on the breeze.

"That was some trick, by the way. Setting your feet on fire, I mean," Truggel said, tapping his fingers reflectively on his broom. Bip winced and continued his examination of the floor. More moments of silence passed unchecked into the atmosphere.

"Did you come to visit your father's grave?" said Truggle finally.

"No," said Bip. "It just seems like a…a waste of time if there's no body in it."

"I always thought it was rather touching that the community made honorary graves for those who chose to venture out into the wilds," Truggle mused.

"My father didn't choose to leave," said Bip glumly. "He just went out to practice some heavy psyence and didn't come back. They said he must have just got lost in a snowstorm."

"Oh really? Is that what they say?" Truggle lit his rank pipe and took a few puffs. "Of course, what would they know?"

Bip looked at the ground for a while, then looked up at the sky. He turned to Truggle and looked into his watery gray eyes. "What?" he said.

"I wonder if it's time for you to learn the truth, my lad."

"The truth about what?" Bip replied.

Truggle blew a thin cloud of smoke, and for a moment, Bip saw a twinkle of intelligence in those old gray eyes that he had never noticed before. "The truth about everything," he said.

THE *SENTINEL* SCREAMED toward the ground, its repellent fields directed entirely around its underbelly and nose. Inside, Finnegun checked their velocity one last time and quickly worked out the probability of surviving such a crash. *It would be fifty per cent,* he thought, *if we weren't heading toward a cliff face and consequently a thousand-foot drop onto a massive lake of ice.*

With an unfathomable *boom,* the craft plunged into the snowy ground, its shielding causing gigantic clods of earth to be ploughed up in front of it. The momentum of the impact sent the vessel crashing through ice and snow toward the sheer cliff face at an alarming rate.

Within the foredeck, Finnegun closed his eyes once again as warning lights flashed and beeped in a rave of panic. *There is no way,* he thought, *that we can possibly slow down in time to avoid sliding over the cliff. Bugger.*

As a sense of finality washed over him, Finnegun opened one of his eyes, determined at least to face his fate head on. He was surprised to see that the landscape had changed slightly; where before there had been an empty expanse between the tobogganing ship and the cliff, there was now a gigantic, oddly shaped snow drift. Finnegun had just enough time to wonder where it had come from before the *Sentinel*, smashing clouds of ice into the air, collided with the mysterious snow drift with an odd suddenness and a sound that can only be described as a colossal *poff!*

Well, that was odd, thought Finnegun. And with that last thought, he blacked out.

Within its icy airbag, the craft gradually slowed and finally stopped, some way from the cliff edge, and began cooling with loud *tinging* noises. There was a long period of stunned silence.

DARKNESS.

A nagging sensation that he had something to be getting on with.

More darkness.

An awareness of cold. A problem in the chronostatic chamber. Not supposed to feel. Pain. Pain in his leg and neck.

Darkness.

"Captain?"

Who, me?

"Captain!"

Five minutes, please.

"Captain, wake up!"

"Muh?" said Finnegun, for the second time that day.

"We made it, sir," Handen said, shaking him. "We're alive!"

"Jolly good," said Finnegun, then groaned as his protesting body began airing a long list of complaints. "Oh dear," he said, wincing. "I think my leg is broken. How is everyone else?"

"We lost two more crew. Defty and Michaelmas. They were killed on impact, sir."

Finnegun nodded. There seemed little else he could do. "Are all the other crew in good shape?"

"A few casualties, Captain, mostly superficial."

"We made it, then?" said Finnegun, a smile spreading across his face for the first time in a few millennia.

"I wouldn't celebrate just yet, Captain," came a voice edged with familiar irritation. "We're buried under tons of snow, and making an exit could be a big problem without looking at a full damage report first. Whatever it was that stopped us going over that cliff has us trapped! And to top it all off, the power's down, and I doubt we have much oxygen left."

"Ah, Izzy." Finnegun smiled sleepily. "I've always admired your optimistic, can-do attitude."

He looked across at the access hatch, which, while open, merely opened onto tons of snow.

"Well, then," said Finnegun, shaking his groggy head, "I suggest that everyone gets into their environment suits and prepares to clear an exit—" He stopped abruptly and cocked his head toward the ceiling. There was an odd thumping sound, like the shuffling of gigantic feet. The crew fell silent as the noise grew louder. After quite some time, a flurry of snow began to cascade into the ship from the access hatch until a hollow was made near the exit. A weak light and a bitter wind swept into the foredeck. Completely against everyone's expectations, a penguin plummeted from the sky and landed with a bang on the ship's deck. It was followed by several others, which proceeded to wallow around in confusion, quacking with the attitude of an animal that has nothing better to do than quack. Finnegun tried to think when he had last seen penguins…

After a few minutes and several more confused penguins, a face dangled from the top of the hatch. A face that Finnegun found disturbingly familiar.

"All right?" said the face.

BOMBING THROUGH SPACE LIKE A BULLET, the Massive Ball of Death twinkled prettily in the light of a nearby sun. Countless years in the coldness of space had left the nuclear cluster dusted with ice, giving it the appearance of a huge and lethal snowball.

In a nearby galactic diner, situated on the third ring of the planet Xarghy'Putput, two Snx' Prtickas sat chewing merrily on Tch' Paknap. They had been hauling a payload of Chifk' kapow back to their home world of CnKTippkle, when they had stopped in the diner for a spot of lunch. FnIk'rrr stared dreamily out of the window, his head resting in one of his twelve hands, while Rrrrrrrrr continued to scoff his Tch' Paknap.

Suddenly FnIk'rrr's facial viewing mesh widened in shock as the Massive Ball of Death zoomed through his field of perception. He could see the enormous destructive potential of the man-made meteor and was alarmed that it was being allowed to roam unchecked through such a widely used transport sector. He tapped his twenty-six fingers nervously and considered telling Rrrrrrrrr about his disturbing discovery. Unfortunately, the Snx'Prticka's language was vastly impractical (as were their seventeen stomachs, their statically charged body hair, and the irrelevant trunks at the smalls of their backs). In the time it would have taken for FnIk'rrr to voice his alarm in the cumbersome Snx'Prticka dialect, the meteor would be long gone. It had taken them three hours merely to order their lunch.

FnIk'rrr tutted loudly through his vocal nostrils (which took several minutes) and once again wished that the Snx'Prticka species wasn't so crap.

The Massive Ball of Death continued to drift through space, accelerating slowly but surely as the gravitational pull of the nearby sun altered its direction by a few degrees.

5

Kaneq: The Beginning and the End

"What?" spluttered Truggle as he flailed his arms and swiveled his head to and fro in confusion.

"I said wake up." Bip sighed. "You fell asleep."

"What? No, I didn't!" replied Truggle, blinking his eyes and yawning hugely.

"Yes, you did. You said something about the truth about everything and then you just fell asleep."

"Really?" muttered Truggle. "Curse my ancient head, I've gone and spoiled a perfectly good dramatic moment."

"Are we quite done here yet?" Bip said, tapping his foot impatiently. "Only I had the rest of the afternoon booked for moping around and such..."

"How long was I asleep?" interrupted Truggle.

"About five minutes?"

"Then we've no time to lose! Quick, lad, follow me!" With an elderly cackle, Truggle began rowing his wheelchair away at a surprising speed, his broom sweeping at the ground like the world's most enthusiastic janitor.

"Wait!" cried Bip. "What's happening? Where are we going? Tell me before you fall asleep again!"

BIP HEAVED for breath as he followed Truggle's chaotic path through the market square. The old man's erratic wheelchair steering, coupled with some well-targeted broom-prodding, was cutting a winding passage through the crowds of revelers. Bip tried his best to keep the rampaging elder in sight. He had never been particularly athletic, preferring slow comfortable paces, or better yet no pace at all, so the unplanned exercise of chasing down a madman's wheelchair was taking its toll on his underused lungs.

Bip had followed the old man's unpredictable chase from the cemetery, past the lumber camps, the farmlands, even the tanning houses and blacksmiths, until, nearly falling over from exhaustion, they had arrived at the market square. What annoyed Bip was that, without the diversions, the market square and the cemetery were only five minutes apart.

Bip had never seen a supermarket, so he had never seen a trolley with a wobbly wheel, and even if he had, he certainly would have never chased a rocket-powered one. Thus, Bip was unable to compare his recent experiences to anything in his personal frame of reference.

Without warning, Bip's stumbling took him into a clearing at the edge of the square where, sitting casually and smoking his long, foul pipe, was Truggle.

"What took you so long?" he chided. Thankfully, Bip's breathless reply was unintelligible to the old man's ears.

"Come along, lad," said the elder cheerfully. "We haven't far to go now."

"Where…are…we…go…ing?" Bip managed.

"Didn't I mention that part?" said Truggle.

"…o," wheezed Bip.

"I'm sure I did," mused Truggle.

"…" said Bip.

"Well, anyway, we're going into the Dome."

Bip choked mid-wheeze. The Dome was one of the few places in the community that was closed to the general public. Only the higher-ranking psyentists and councilmen were allowed access to the mysterious building on the outskirts of Kaneq... and the elders, of course. The contents of what was rumored to be Kaneq's oldest building were kept a deep secret. Even the most friendly and carefree of those who were allowed access would turn quiet and withdrawn if their friends enquired about the Dome's significance. Of all the chosen elite who were allowed access to the Dome, and all the worthy who were not, it seemed wrong for Bip to be invited to enter on the whim of someone who was quite possibly insane. Even so, as Truggle wheeled away, Bip could not help but follow, his curiosity overriding his sense of duty.

AFTER ONLY A FEW MINUTES' walk, following a surprisingly coherent and straightforward route set by Truggle, Bip found himself at one of the few portal points in Kaneq's heatshield. Far on the opposite side of the shimmering barrier, he could see the distant snowy mound of the Dome.

It was not considered wise to attempt to enter Kaneq by simply walking straight though the heatshield (unless you wanted a really, *really* deep tan), so exit and entrance points were set up sporadically for the few occasions when a citizen might want access to the rest of the Ice Plains. The dangers of going too close to the heatshield were stressed to Kaneqians from an early age, and its value for keeping the unwanted elements outside far outweighed the occasional fatality for those inside who would do anything for a laugh. As he approached the portal point, Bip could feel the uncomfortably hot temperature of the transparent heat wall, even though they were still some distance from it.

The two psyentists manning the portal point hesitated slightly when they saw Bip, but one nod from Truggle sent them immediately into action. They concentrated on the equation that would allow a thin gap to appear in the shield and grant access to the Dome. A faint shimmer and a loud fizzing noise were the only indication that part of the colossal force field was being drawn aside like a huge, boiling curtain. A third psyentist came up to Bip and offered him a very thick coat, fashioned from the woolly hide of the snowcow, with huge gloves and a tight hood sewn into the heavy fabric. Bip had a brief moment to wonder what the coat was for before an icy wind, the likes of which he had never experienced, blasted cruelly from the slowly appearing portal.

The Kaneqians deemed it a necessity that the community should experience at least some of the winter season. For a few months every year, a tolerable amount of ice and snow was allowed into the village. Bip, in his childhood, had thoroughly enjoyed building snowmen and chucking snowballs with the other kids in the brief winter spells. However, the season that lived just meters from the cozy embrace of the ever-burning heatshield was not a light-hearted reminder of the frivolities of winter's play. No. It was a harsh, slapping cold that tore into the bone and into the soul. Bip clutched at his body, shivering madly and immediately re-evaluating his decision to follow Truggle.

"A bit nippy, isn't it?" said Truggle. "I should wrap up if I were you."

Bip clambered into the cumbersome coat and relished the tiny relief it gave. They waited while an obliging psyentist tied some worn-out skis onto Truggle's wheelchair then ushered them out into the cold.

Bip looked around at the vast expanse of the Ice Plains and experienced an odd conflict of agoraphobia and claustrophobia. Having spent most of his life in the familiarity of the village, the unreachable horizons and towering mountains of the icy wilderness he now faced were intimidating to say the least, but the thick whirling of the constant snow seemed to muffle sound, vision, and distance, adding an uncomfortable sense of restriction to the cold panorama.

It was only a few short minutes' walk to the Dome, which Truggle spent merrily gliding through the snowdrifts, singing an old drinking song in a gruff tenor. The minutes were not so carefree for Bip, however, as he trudged pathetically through the overwhelming elements, blinking away the stinging ice that was continually thrown into his eyes. The moisture in the air forced him to remove his glasses, meaning that the white blindness around him was even more blurred than before. Bip gave a sigh of relief that turned to cold steam before him as they approached the Dome.

The building reminded Bip of the igloo he had turned Michaelmas's house into, though on a much larger scale. He briefly wondered how much effort it would take to make a mistake resulting in an igloo as large as the Dome. Then he wondered miserably if he was capable of making it.

Suddenly, Bip realized that the raging winds around him had calmed somewhat and that the temperature had warmed slightly.

"Another heatshield," called Truggle from ahead, by way of explanation. "Not a big one, mind. It keeps the entrance clear." He pointed to a large funnel in the snow that led downward and seemingly underneath the dome.

"Follow me!" he cried merrily, and slid down the funnel into an all-embracing darkness. Bip heard the slight echo of an old man's voice saying, "Wheeeee!"

Gulping back his doubts and considering the alternative of a harsh walk back to Kaneq, Bip slid down the funnel.

FROM SOME DISTANCE AWAY, a beast watched as Bip disappeared from view. It watched and thought about killing. The beast was a grubear, one of the most ferocious creatures to stalk the snowbound tundra of the Ice Plains. Standing nearly seven feet at the shoulder, the grubear's shaggy, white hide was crisscrossed with scars from territorial battles and the occasional challenging prey. It was old and tough, one of the most revered hunter-killers even amongst its own competitive kind, but for some reason, it had left its normal hunting territories, leaving them vulnerable to ambitious rivals. For days now, it had stalked an unspecific but all-consuming hunger, fueled by the strange nagging whisper in the back of its mind that had convinced it to give up its hard-won champion status and venture into unknown territory. Now, finally, the grubear had found the source of the unexplained need to kill. It stared hungrily at Bip's disappearing frame and listened briefly to the maddening whispers in its head. It knew what had to be done.

If the beast had not been so intent on the unusual messages it was receiving and had paid more attention to its innate ability to sense fluctuations in the surrounding magnetic field, it would certainly have detected the presence of the monster behind it. Unfortunately, even if the grubear had been able to detect the threat, it was massively outmatched. A fist the size of boulder slammed down onto the oblivious beast's back, snapping its spine, and instantly ending its life. The grubear stood stock still for a moment, then fell heavily to the ground. What had been a magnificent animal mere seconds ago was now just a lifeless carcass, splayed and broken in the snow. The assailant lifted its massive fist from the rapidly cooling corpse and absentmindedly rubbed its gory knuckles on its chest. Then it paused, tilted its huge, hairy head, and listened carefully to the incessant whispering at the back of its mind.

BIP BLINKED RAPIDLY, trying to adjust his eyes to the gloom. The slide down the funnel had been uneventful, starting rapidly then slowing smoothly to a halt in the room he now stood in. Peering into the darkness, Bip hoped for some clue as to the shape of the strange cavern. He took a step forward and was unnerved to hear his footstep echo with a metallic ring.

Without warning, an eerie glow began to illuminate the darkness around him. The light had a misty quality and emanated from no source Bip could locate. Soon the light was bright enough for him to get a grasp of his surroundings. He gasped. The room was the largest indoor space he had ever seen. The ceiling stretched too high into the darkness for him to see it, and the walls and floor seemed to merge into one cylindrical curve. More impressive than the sheer scale of the room was the fact that it seemed to be constructed entirely of a metallic substance. Metal was not uncommon in Kaneq, being used in everything from plumbing pipes to cutlery, but the mining and processing of the scarce metals in the surrounding Ice Plains was too costly a process to encourage a large demand. The Kaneqians, with their carefully controlled environment, were quite happy to construct most things from the more easily attainable wood sources within the perimeter of the heatshield. Bip had never seen much metal in one place before, and the room he found himself in now seemed horribly alien to his sensibilities.

"Welcome to the Dome," said Truggle, his cracked voice resonating harshly. Bip, who had been staring in awe at the ceiling, very nearly fell over in shock. It seemed that Truggle had come from nowhere.

"Come along, lad, we can't be standing around gawking all day." With that, Truggle wheeled his chair slightly backward, causing a disc of white light to appear on the floor. Bip stepped backward hesitantly.

"What is this place?" he breathed.

Truggle sucked thoughtfully at his gums. "Well, put it like this; you've seen the fishers who head down to the frozen lake now and then?"

"Yes."

"And you know that, sometimes, when the season is right, they go out into the sea on boats?"

Bip nodded. He had seen boats, but only as they were constructed, never afloat.

"Well, that's sort of what this is," said Truggle, gesturing to the walls around them. "This is a really, really big boat."

Bip frowned doubtfully.

"Trust me, that's the best way I can explain it. Now, come over here."

Bip started hesitantly toward the glowing area of floor.

"Come along—there's nothing to be afraid of," said Truggle.

For the second time that day, Bip took a leap of faith and stepped onto the quietly pulsating disc. He nearly screamed in terror as the disc suddenly plummeted downward. Truggle poked him reassuringly with his broom. "It's an elevator, lad. It's like a ladder but faster."

Bip nodded and tried to calm down, but his terror was not so easily dismissed as they fell into the unknown. Unlike the room they had come from, the corridor surrounding the elevator was oppressively close. It was hard to judge their rate of descent, although occasionally an odd glow would zip past them toward the ceiling at high speed. The only sound Bip could hear was the faint *swish* of the traveling disc moving through the air.

"Am I dreaming?" he whispered.

"What are you whispering for?" replied Truggle. "This place is huge! You can talk as loudly as you like!" He demonstrated by screaming in Bip's face.

"Don't you feel a little overwhelmed?" said Bip when the echoes had died down.

"Nah. You get used to it," said Truggle "You get used to pretty much everything when you're as old as I am."

As they descended, the tight corridor gave way rapidly until they were entering a room that, while not as big as the one they had come from, was still enormous by Bip's standards. He was slightly relieved, and a little surprised, to see that the room was filled with people, all of them hurrying back and forth from various tasks. The room was also filled with more metal contraptions, many of which twinkled with random lights or made the occasional whirring sound. Bip could see no purpose to the various metal boxes, but many of the people below seemed to be regarding them with great interest.

As the disc came to a smooth halt in the center of the room, Bip was surprised by how many of the people he recognized. Whether it was from the tavern or merely passing them in the street, the various faces of the Kaneqian elite were all familiar to Bip. Here, in this alien environment, he had expected to find something different from the everyday citizens of Kaneq.

"This is the archive," said Truggle. "This is where we keep the ancient wisdom, in case you've ever wondered."

"So it is true?" Bip gasped. "There is an ancient wisdom?"

"Well, not so much wisdom," mused Truggle, "but certainly information. Lots and lots of information. Some of it far too complex to tell us anything useful, but some of it...well, some of it very useful indeed."

"Where do you keep it all?" said Bip, craning his neck, searching the large but mostly empty room.

"In these metal boxes," Truggle said, banging one of the contraptions with his broom for emphasis. Bip was unimpressed; on the occasions when he had given any thought to the legendary "ancient wisdom" he had envisioned dusty tomes of rotting leather, stacked ceiling-high in some neglected catacomb. The flashing box, as pretty as it was, seemed a bit of a let-down.

"They're called computers," said Truggle. "They're sort of a big library in a little box. Well, more like lots of big libraries in a box, really. We don't fully understand how they work anymore. They're a relic of our ancestors, the founders."

"The founders?" Bip's prior disappointment dissipated dispassionately. Information about the pilgrims who had decided to build Kaneq in the middle of a desolate wasteland was vague at best, stating only that they had come from a far-off land to make a new home. Bip, like many other Kaneqians, had always been curious about why the founders had chosen to live in such isolation.

"The founders, yes," said Truggle, rubbing his hairy chin reflectively. "Yes, I suppose that's the best place to start. At the beginning, I mean." He rowed himself over to one of the computers, this one looking no different from the rest but for a contraption that resembled a large and intricate pair of goggles, which Truggle gestured for Bip to look into. Bip, figuring that he had gone along with everything else so far, looked into the goggles without hesitation.

"Now this might feel a bit funny..." said Truggle, and Bip felt his brain being sucked through his eyeballs.

LIGHT. A million spectrums of multidimensional light. Solid light. Breathing light. Light that looked like sound. Sound that felt like light. A sense of time passing. Passing the wrong way. A feeling of incredible speed. Bip opened his eyes.

CAPTAIN FINNEGUN OPENED HIS EYES. He wiped the sweat from his brow and surveyed the handiwork of the combined efforts of the *Sentinel*'s Elite-Gifted. What before had been a blizzard-soaked stretch of certain death had been transformed into merely miles of dead countryside. The heatshield equation, especially at this scale, was difficult to initiate but easy to maintain once established. Finnegun relaxed and turned his attention to other matters. He tried to take a step and stumbled slightly. It wasn't just the cold that made this new land hard going; owing to the planet's size and density, the gravity was stronger than he was used to. It would be a trial just walking around until his muscles adapted. He sighed. Another inconvenience in an already *very* inconvenient situation.

After the crash landing, they had decided to leave the *Sentinel* outside the perimeter of the heatshield, buried under the tons of snow, lest it attract the attention of any locals who might not appreciate extra-terrestrials in their back garden. Finnegun had thought the possibility of meeting anyone on the icy continent unlikely at best, but the stranger who had rescued the crew had insisted that they prepare for a long stay, and in turn, Handen had insisted on the various security procedures designed for this particular turn of events.

Finnegun allowed his mind to dwell on their odd rescuer for a while. The stranger had disappeared, rather mysteriously, soon after explaining that he thought it was extremely doubtful that the captain and his crew would be able to leave the ice continent in the near future. He had been right. Even now the engineers and technicians were trying to salvage any useful components from the *Sentinel*, but the main engine laid scattered in fragments on a mountaintop several miles away. There was no question that the crew would have to survive on the seemingly lifeless ice continent for quite a while. Erecting the heatshield had been a good start to the long process of bunking down in a hostile environment.

The captain thought back to the face of the stranger who had helped them in their time of need. His striking familiarity was still an intriguing mystery, and although Finnegun had formulated several conclusions as to the rescuer's origin, none of them were relevant to the situation at hand. He would file his suspicions away for later consideration.

Finnegun turned at the sound of approaching footsteps. It was Izzy, her flustered features looking more flustered than usual.

"It's bloody freezing out there," she grumbled, shaking the snow from her spiky head.

Finnegun allowed himself a small smile. "I would have thought that after so many millennia in stasis you would appreciate the feel of a real atmosphere again," he mused.

"A beach would have been nice," Izzy snapped, "but for preference anywhere but here would have been lovely."

"How's the salvage going?" said Finnegun

"We have most of the provisions, various tools, various materials we can recycle. Long term data storage is available for read only access, and probably will be for the foreseeable future. It's one of the few useful systems that relies on the secondary reserve batteries."

"Communications?"

"Down. We tried to bypass them to available power sources, but the danger of an overload is too great. The Mother Tongue survived intact, but without the appropriate amplification relays we've no hope of sending any more sub-space messages. Or even deep-space messages, for that matter."

"I wouldn't worry about it, Izzy; if the message was received, they will come for us. If not, they know where we are."

The two stood for a while, watching the rest of the Elite-Gifted as they began to cultivate the dead land within the heatshield, encouraging life wherever they could find it.

"I'm sorry about Kanick," said Finnegun, after a while. "I know you and he were—"

"He did what was…necessary," said Izzy, not looking up from the ground.

"Even so…" said Finnegun.

"Even so…" Izzy agreed.

The two Clarions stood awhile, gently steaming as the snow melted from their shoulders.

"We buried him along with Defty and Michaelmas," said Izzy, sighing heavily.

Finnegun nodded his approval. Though the remains of the three crew members who had given their lives for the survival of their shipmates had been evaporated along with the main engine, the honorary grave and ceremony was very typical of the Clarion people, who would treat and tend the graves as though they contained the mortal remains of their lost comrades.

Finnegun pretended not to notice as Izzy sniffed loudly and walked away. He would have liked to say something comforting, but there were many things to be done and there would be time to mourn later.

He thought again about the mysterious stranger who had helped them in their time of need. He thought about one of the various conclusions he had reached and took a laser pen from his top pocket. Bending down, grunting slightly with the unaccustomed effort, he picked up one of the smaller debris fragments of the ship's hull and began to burn a message into it with meticulous handwriting. It was possible that the information on the ship's computers would remain accessible for centuries to come, even without primary power, but sometimes it was best to put faith in more tangible and traditional forms of communication.

He began the letter with, "To whom it may concern..."

TO WHOM IT MAY CONCERN...

A long time ago, further back than the birth of the oldest sun, there were sides to pick. Two sides to the basic conflict. Before there was war, there was always order and chaos, and those who knew this chose their sides.

And the sides competed.

Many ages ago we, the Clarion people, looked to the stars and wondered if there was other life in the universe. We reached out nervously with signals and ships to discover if we were alone in existence and, in a moment that would define our history, we made Contact. Suddenly the universe was a more interesting place. Our reality had changed. Our existence had been redefined. We looked upon the stars and knew we were not alone. Soon, we had bridged our tiny solar system with a wondrous and intriguing intergalactic community of uncountable alien souls, and in doing so had opened our minds to information beyond our imagination...

It was then that we learned of the sides and the conflict, then that we learned of the Caretakers and the Discordance; those who defended order and those who actively sought chaos. It was then that we learnt of the Choice, something that all civilizations will eventually encounter. We were obligated to decide whether we believed order should be protected and nurtured in the ultraverse, or whether unfettered chaos is the natural and proper state of things, in which no life form has the right to interfere. Being what we were and believing what we did, we chose order, joining many other species and uniting in a common and simple goal: to protect less evolved life forms from the forces of adverse randominity, the shadows of those who would see order disrupted.

There were other factions across the ultraverse, other subgroups and divisions. There were the Indifferents, the Interferers, the Headstarters, the Optimists, the Harshliners, the Resounding Yessers, the Nearsayers, the Old Guards and the New Pop Fallacy and many, many more. But the alliance that dedicated itself purely to protecting order called themselves the Caretakers.

The Caretakers would use their powers and technology to watch over less developed species, keeping them safe from the harsh surprises of the ultraverse until they were better able to decide their own destiny, as we had so long ago. We took it upon ourselves to watch over worlds until they could make the Choice, and regardless of what they chose, we believe that to live long enough to realize this choice is the right of every civilization.

Now to the matter at hand...

It was the duty of the Clarions, and specifically the crew of the Sentinel, to ensure that the planet of Bersch reached an appropriate level of maturity without interference from hostile outside forces. Unfortunately, due to circumstances outside our expectations, the Sentinel is now unable to defend the planet of Bersch. In a thousand years' time, from this day, Bersch will be utterly destroyed by a powerful astral disaster.

It is my hope that Clarion reservists will arrive in time to intervene. Until then, the mission of the Sentinel remains the same: we must attempt to protect Bersch, or at the very least warn its inhabitants of the impending danger.

I am unsure how long my crew will be stranded, or how soon we will be able to warn the planet's inhabitants of their precarious situation. For now, we will remain, as always, Caretakers.

CAPTAIN JULIUS FINNEGUN. EG.
 The SS Sentinel

6

Big Fat Responsibilities

Bip reeled and stumbled back from the goggles, the nauseating feeling of existing in two places making his head spin wildly. He reached out to steady himself and found only the floor for support.

It was too much information. Not only was there life outside Kaneq—he had always been led to expect as much—but life outside the planet, the *galaxy*!

Bip's vision spun erratically as he tried to process the unfathomable. The images he had seen had been real, he knew it as surely as he knew his legs existed, although he quickly reconsidered that analogy as his knees turned to jelly and he sprawled face-down on the cold metallic floor.

Caretakers, Order, the truth about everything… Bip screamed for a while then threw up before slipping into blissful unconsciousness.

"Just once," said Truggle, after the commotion had died down, "I wish they'd take it with a little more nonchalance."

DARKNESS.

A nagging sensation that he had something to be getting on with.

These aren't my memories.

More darkness.

An awareness of cold. A problem in the chronostatic chamber. Not supposed to feel.

What's a chronostatic chamber?

Pain. Pain in his leg and neck.

These aren't my memories. There is no pain.

Darkness.

"Bip?"

Who, me?

"Bip!"

Five minutes, please.

"Bip, wake up!"

"Muh?" said Bip, and wondered where he'd last heard the expression.

"It's all right, boy," said a familiar cracked voice. "I'm here."

"I had the strangest dreams," murmured Bip.

"Hah! No, not quite, lad. You had the strangest reality!"

Bip sat up suddenly and blinked rapidly as his eyes readjusted to the gloom. The first sight to greet him was the horrible grin of Truggle's withered face.

"Oh no," he muttered. "It was all real, wasn't it?"

"Hah! Well done, lad," said Truggle, his laugh snapping like a gun shot. "Usually people try to deny the inevitable for a touch longer, but I see you're ready to get on with things—"

Truggle was cut off by the sound of Bip throwing up again.

"Maybe not, then," he concluded. He fished around in his heavy robes for a while until he produced what looked like a piece of scrap metal. "I usually have a speech prepared to convince people that what they've seen is real, but I've found that this is a much easier way of getting the message across." He threw the piece of scrap metal at Bip's feet. It had eroded slightly with the years, but was still instantly recognizable to Bip as Captain Finnegun's message. Bip couldn't help but believe in its authenticity—he had, in effect, been there when it was written. He looked up at Truggle for an explanation.

"What you saw," Truggle began, "was something like a memory—a diary entry but with pictures and sounds and emotions. As I said, we're not sure how it works, but the important thing is that now you know the truth. You know the reason why every man, woman, and child in Kaneq is here."

"I did wonder," Bip croaked.

"But the question on your lips, I should imagine, is 'What on Bersch has this got to do with me?'"

Bip nodded, still too busy spitting away the taste of vomit to answer.

"Well, Bip," said Truggle, cheerfully, "I hate to be the bearer of big fat responsibilities, but you're going to save the world."

Bip nodded. Then he threw up again.

CAPTAIN'S LOG. Day Fourteen.

I am beginning to wonder if the stranger's assessment of our situation was really as bleak as he made it seem.

His exact words were, "I wouldn't expect to leave this place any time soon," though part of me hopes he was exaggerating. Of course, another part of me wonders how far a man who disappeared without a trace should be trusted.

However, these musings are not useful to our current dilemma.

The establishment of a temporary base on the ice continent is accelerating at a very satisfactory rate. The crew has managed to construct barracks from surplus materials salvaged from the ship's wreckage and the Elite-Gifted have managed to encourage the growth of various useful plants and foliage within the boundaries of the heatshield.

Although food stock is, at present, abundant, we consider it wise to prepare for all possibilities. To this end, Handen has suggested forming a "hunting and scavenging" party—though I daresay he is having great difficulty explaining the processes involved to the rest of the crew. Currently he is taking aside those with "hostility potential" for extensive training in "aggressive survival behavior." What this means I have no idea, but I trust Handen's judgment…

FINNEGUN PUT down the wrist console and tapped the stylus on his teeth. He was glad the technicians had been able to update data storage for minimal input functions. At least if their mission failed utterly, they would have a detailed log of their progress that might be useful to other Clarions who found themselves in similar situations. Also, though Finnegun didn't like to admit it, the log was good for his morale. It helped him to believe that soon there would be someone to read it. He turned as footsteps approached. It was Izzy, ready with her progress report.

"You'll be pleased to know we now have plumbing in the barracks." She smiled smugly.

"Fantastic," said Finnegun with a grin. "I was beginning to wonder if we'd smell this bad for the rest of our time here."

"I've been thinking," began Izzy, reproach evident in her usually confident voice, "about what we're going to call our temporary home."

Finnegun looked out at the colossal mountains they had narrowly avoided during their landing. "I thought 'Kanick' might be appropriate," he said.

"I thought so as well," said Izzy. "Thank you."

Finnegun continued to look at the mountains as Izzy walked away. Tomorrow he would talk to Handen about the progress made with his hunting party.

BIP SAT in his usual secluded table at the Empty Goat and thought hard. For the first time in quite a while he had something very hard to think about. In less than a year, the world would end. All his friends, family, and the people he didn't care much about but didn't want to see obliterated, would be…well, obliterated. In less than a year.

Bip pulled hard at his tankard of ale. He had no desire to get drunk, but a strong desire not to think.

He had been shocked by how many people knew about Bersch's impending disaster and the true purpose and origin of the Kaneqians. That Dunman and Truggle were at the heart of the conspiracy hadn't been too surprising, but when he'd found out that Michaelmas and even his own mother were in on it, he'd been quite upset. He'd been even more upset to learn that he wasn't the first person chosen to "save the world." Since the crash landing, every generation had thrown up people who would venture into the wilderness in an attempt to reach civilization. As the community had settled and the original founders had grown old, the knowledge of Kaneq's true purpose had been entrusted to certain individuals who would pass it down the generations to the present day's inner circle of trustees. Thus, from every generation, a candidate was selected to leave the community and make the dangerous journey to find and make contact with other peoples. These candidates were rarely heard from again, the success or failure of their mission never disclosed.

Bip pulled hard at the tankard again. Selected candidates hardly ever refused the mission once they were told the truth, Truggle had told him. Bip could see why. Firstly, if the world is going to end and you're given a chance of saving it, there is a very strong moral obligation to comply, especially if it's the world you happen to be standing on at the time. Secondly, if you didn't at least try, you would get some very scathing looks from everybody when the world did end.

These reasons were all very well and good, but the clincher for Bip was when he'd learned that his father had been a previous candidate. He'd had a very long and tearful conversation with his mother and Michaelmas about the true fate of his father, after which he had been first outraged at being lied to, then later quietly proud. It had turned out that Bip's family line had a long history of selected candidates, dating back to the early volunteers. He had understood, eventually, why he had never been told the truth about his father. The knowledge of Bersch's appointment with annihilation was best kept from the general public, as people don't tend to sleep well if they think the planet is going to explode. He also understood why Michaelmas couldn't keep his promise about offering him work. There would, after all, not have been any point. As a sort of apology, the drinks were entirely on Michaelmas for the evening, of which Bip was taking full advantage.

The question that still bothered him a lot was why he had been picked instead of anyone else. Truggle had admitted that there were far more qualified candidates but professed his faith in Bip's psyentific potential and adaptability to new situations.

"Turning a house into an igloo," he had said, obviously having been informed of the botched home improvement by Michaelmas, "is no easy feat. There's definite potential in you, lad. You just need a bit of a kick in the bum."

Even this argument hadn't convinced Bip, who knew that if he were picking a savior of the planet, he would look a lot further afield than himself. Eventually Truggle had confessed, in a roundabout manner, that sometimes candidates were picked purely on gut instinct. This had not instilled Bip with confidence.

Truggle had attempted to reassure him, stating that he wouldn't be thrown into the wilderness unprepared and would be trained vigorously for a solid month. Bip, who had already made peace with his lack of physical motivation, winced hard at words like "trained" and "vigorously." He had winced harder when he had been introduced to his "personal trainer," a bear of a man called Rynford, whose square jaw, steely gaze, and amazingly intimidating moustache Bip had only ever seen lurking at the back of council meetings. Rynford was Kaneq's Huntmaster, and like all the hunters, he was surly, secretive, and had more muscle than could possibly be convenient. Bip had never got on with the hunters, who forsook the Kaneqian lifestyle of fairly docile contentment for a life of danger exploring the surrounding wilderness and scouting for possible hostile animal or monster activity. Rynford had taken one look at Bip and insisted that the training begin at dawn the next day, which had made Bip wince so hard his face had nearly fallen off.

Bip sighed his well-practiced, forlorn sigh. He had never wanted anything more than a quiet, easy life, but it seemed the universe was conspiring to make this a laughable impossibility. He emptied his tankard and was surprised to see it replaced almost immediately. He looked up into the broad face of Bailey, who was going through one of his rare phases of being neither drunk nor hungover.

"What's up with your face?" said Bailey. "You look like you've got the weight of the world on your shoulders."

Bip pulled hard on his new tankard. "Sod off, Bailey," he said.

BIP WAS EXHAUSTED. He was past exhausted. If he'd had any energy left, he would have invented whole new words for just how exhausted he was.

Dawn had been merely an hour ago, and already he wanted to go back to bed.

He had been sleeping, quite peacefully, when the first rays of morning sunshine had sidled through his curtains. Before he had even had time to acknowledge the new day, his bedroom door had crashed open and he had been lifted bodily from his bed and placed in a freezing cold shower in what had seemed like only a few blurred and terrible seconds. When he had finally recovered from the shock and got his bearings, he had looked up into the wide grin of Rynford.

"Time to get up," he had said. "We're going out for breakfast."

So far, "going out for breakfast" had consisted of an hour-long jog through the endless snowdrifts of the Ice Plains.

Bip panted, struggling against the weight of his insulating leathers and the quick pace of the athletic Huntmaster, whose flapping furs and long spear could be seen racing ahead through the constant blizzard. Bip's knees had long since turned to rubber, and he had begun to lag farther and farther behind Rynford—which was not encouraging as he had no idea where he was or, for that matter, *who* he was anymore. His whole body burned with effort, which seemed odd because various extremities were telling him it was very cold indeed. Freezing, actually.

With a heaving sigh, Bip fell face-first into the snow and wondered if anyone would mind if he just fell asleep for a little while. He was jerked from his thoughts of slumber by the rough grip of Rynford, who hauled him from the ground and held him up easily by the collar.

"Aye, I think that'll do for a warmup, lad. Time for a bit of breakfast, I'm thinking."

Bip blinked rapidly and waited for his breath to steady before saying, "What are you on about, you muscle-headed madman? We're in the middle of nowhere!" At least, that was what he meant to say. What he actually said was, "Whu? *Cough cough...COUGH!*"

Rynford pointed to a patch of snow that looked pretty much like every other patch of snow. "Driftdiggers," he said, with a hint of smugness.

Bip looked confused for a moment before understanding slapped him with the fingers of doom. A driftdigger was a vicious breed of mammal, akin to a giant carnivorous gopher, whose main method of hunting was to burrow under prey and eat them from beneath while they were off balance. Bip had heard many deeply nasty campfire stories about encounters with driftdiggers; the fact that they were all based on fact was less than reassuring.

"We can't eat driftdiggers!" he wailed. "Driftdiggers eat people, not the other way around!"

"Nonsense!" Rynford snorted. "You can eat just about anything if you put your mind to it."

Bip was momentarily flabbergasted, unsure whether Rynford was deliberately ignoring reason or just trying to upset him. "The point I'm trying to make is, yeah? The message I'm trying to convey here is, right? We'll be killed. That really is the be-all and end-all of it. We'll be killed. Horribly."

"That's a very negative attitude, laddie, and besides..." Rynford turned a stern gaze to his young trainee. "Where you're going, chances are there are a few worse things than a glorified gopher."

Bip looked glumly at the ground while this harsh observation sank in.

"And anyway," continued Rynford, "there's good meat on one of them buggers."

Bip looked thoughtful for a moment. He was cold, and he was tired, but it was starting to dawn on him that he was also very, very hungry.

"So how do you go about killing a driftdigger, then?" he asked.

Rynford bent down and dug up a rock from under the snow. "Strength, skill, ingenuity, cunning, and..." he carefully weighed the ice-bound rock in his massive fists, "something to hit them with."

BIP WATCHED from afar as Rynford casually approached the driftdigger's lair, his spear held nonchalantly over one shoulder and the newly acquired rock concealed in one of his various leather satchels.

For a while, nothing seemed to happen. The endless whistle of the blizzard was the only sound. The rolling ocean of snow remained undisturbed by erupting monsters. Bip felt an awful twist in his guts as the snowdrift Rynford was approaching first shuddered and then, with a rumble and creak, collapsed. The deep rumbling continued as the ground between where the drift had been and Rynford began to shake and subside. It was clear that the driftdigger had sensed the Huntmaster's presence and was moving in for the kill.

Bip bit his knuckles in terror as Rynford stood stock still, his spear ready in hand, awaiting the onslaught of the beast. Bip couldn't help but think how small and inadequate the once-mighty Rynford seemed compared to the wave of menace that approached him. He wanted to call out but could not, could only watch helplessly as the driftdigger moved closer and closer until it was very nearly on top of the Huntmaster. Just when Bip had thought Rynford truly done for, the big man plunged his spear into the ground and vaulted his body high into the air, narrowly avoiding the erupting muzzle of the driftdigger. Time seemed to slow as the giant beast's head reared up in an explosion of ice to snatch the arcing hunter out of the sky with teeth liked razored tombstones. Bip even had time to see the wicked red glint in the creature's beady, ferret-like eyes, shining like a firework in the surrounding palette of white. But the monster's actions were halted unexpectedly. Just as the driftdigger seemed set to devour Rynford, it stopped suddenly, finding its jaws jammed open by the length of the Huntmaster's spear. Rynford, with an astonishing feat of muscular control, balanced calmly on the shaft of his spear, the sturdy piece of wood the only thing between him and the wet, gaping maw of the monster beneath him. Quickly but carefully, Rynford reached into a satchel and pulled out the rock he had picked up earlier. With little ceremony, threw it into the Driftdigger's throat. Then he ran along his spear and flipped gracefully from the creature's nose as it began to slowly choke to death.

Bip realized he was still biting his knuckles. He had drawn blood.

"AND THAT," Rynford said, "is how we get breakfast."

They had found shelter in one of the Ice Plains' many cubbies and caves and were enjoying some small relief from the cold provided by a fire Rynford had made. One of the useful benefits of a driftdigger's carcass was that the natural oils in its pelt were conveniently flammable, meaning that both trainer and trainee could reap the benefits of a warm, if stinky, fire.

Bip had been quietly nauseated when Rynford had taken out a long dagger and begun carving the useful meat from the defeated beast, bagging and burying what they couldn't carry and taking as much of the pelt as possible, which had a number of other uses in Kaneq, such as providing lamp oil and lubricants. When Rynford had carefully removed the slab-like front teeth, Bip had been confused.

"Personal collection," Rynford had explained. "I've nearly got enough to tile my house with."

Despite how queasy the butchery of the animal had made him, Bip couldn't help but salivate at the smell of the thin strips of meat that Rynford was now carefully roasting over the fire.

"Of course, driftdigger always tastes better with a fried egg,"

Rynford muttered distractedly as he handed Bip a lump of sizzling meat on the end of a stick. "There's nothing like a couple of fried eggs to make up a good breakfast."

Bip nodded dumbly and began munching on the cut of meat, finding great satisfaction in both the succulence and the warmth of the food. He chewed happily as warm juice trickled down his chin.

"So, then," said Rynford, after a while. "What are you killing for breakfast tomorrow?"

Bip paused mid-mouthful, his eyes widening. "Sorry?" he said.

"Well, I'm supposed to be training you, you know. Saving the world and all that, you remember? Today I showed you how to get breakfast in the wild—tomorrow I want to see how much you picked up."

For a long while Bip couldn't think of anything to say, still unsure whether or not the big Huntmaster was exercising his robust and sadistic sense of humor.

"I'm sorry, Rynford," he concluded finally. "I don't think I can do what you did."

"Oh, you mean all the back-flips and whatever? That's mainly just for show, laddie, you don't have to—"

"No, you don't understand," interrupted Bip. "I don't think I could kill anything. It just seems a bit…well, cruel, really."

Rynford stared for a while, a muscle in his cheek twitching rhythmically. Bip couldn't figure out whether the big man was angry or thoughtful and could only wait as the Huntmaster's trail of thought reached its conclusion. Finally, Rynford let out a short sigh before saying, "Look, lad. I don't want to seem pushy or anything, but I've got to prepare you for the worst. As far as I'm concerned, there is only one priority in the wilderness, one golden rule that every hunter should remember, and that is, don't get eaten."

Bip sat for a while. "I think I can remember that one," he said.

"No, no, lad. It might seem fairly obvious, but you'd be surprised by the number of people I tell that to who go out and get themselves eaten. They might die of exposure first, or starvation, or from falling off a cliff, but sooner or later something eats them. So here's what I do to get around it, see? If I think something's going to eat me, I eat it first." Rynford leaned back smugly. "Top o' the food chain, see? It's harder to eat something that's eating you right back. Law of the wild."

Bip thought for a while. "So what you're saying is, if I think something is going to eat me, I should eat it first?"

Rynford grinned widely. "Aye, that's right! It's a metaphor for the whole of aggressive survival behavior in one. There's beasties out there with more teeth than brain cells, and they're all just itching for an easy lunch. The defenseless are nothing but wafer-thin mints in the delicatessen of the wilderness. The trick is to grow your own teeth: cunning, intelligence, skill! The trick is to become the diner, not the dinner!"

"You mean it's a dog-eat-dog world, sort of thing?"

"Aye, I suppose. Though I'll eat pretty much anything, to tell you the truth."

FROM SOME DISTANCE AWAY, the monster watched the soft glow of the fire that was nearly lost in the brightness of the surrounding snow. It watched and thought about killing. The monster was a yeti, and with its masses of matted white hair, it blended quite easily into the landscape of the Ice Plains. It was often mistaken for a large hill, or sometimes a small mountain. This sometimes meant that, instead of wasting energy hunting, it could simply wait around all day for some unsuspecting creature to try to use it as shelter. It rested its weight on its giant fists and thought about the best way to kill the little man peoples who were currently eating the tooth beastie.

The yeti hadn't been intimidated by the larger man people's display of skill in killing the tooth beastie—the yeti could have dispatched it in half the time, and with a lot less showing-off involved to boot—but a gut feeling stayed the monster's urge to attack. Though the yeti wasn't the brightest of monsters, it had a wary sense of cunning that told it that attacking two of the man peoples might not be to its advantage. It had seen man peoples in action before and knew them to be swift, intelligent hunters who would retaliate in large numbers if openly threatened.

The yeti momentarily put a hand over its ears. The maddening whisper that was urging the monster to attack was becoming more persistent every day. It was starting to affect the creature's judgment. Part of the monster's animal brain wondered why it was taking such an interest in killing these particular man peoples, who had very little meat and were more trouble than they were worth. The constant whispering at the back of its mind scattered these thoughts, leaving the yeti with a simple and unquestionable desire to kill.

With one last glance over at the man peoples' position, the yeti lumbered off into the white. It was a patient beast and would return when the odds were more to its liking.

BIP STUMBLED into his room and stood briefly in the doorway, relishing being indoors. Then he staggered across the floor and landed in a heap on his bed. He was too cold and tired to run a bath, too exhausted to make any supper. Bip curled up under his duvet and moaned aloud.

He had thought that after the slaying of the driftdigger, the rest of his first training day might be a little less extreme. He had been proved horribly wrong. Rynford's boundless energy had allowed for only a short break after breakfast, after which they had taken another jog through the freezing cold to a short cliff face, where Rynford had taught Bip the benefit of "not falling to an icy grave" by forcing him to climb the slippery rocks with only a few daggers for support and a thin rope that Rynford held as his only insurance against a messy death. If that experience hadn't been traumatic enough, three hours of intense weapons training had left Bip a nervous wreck. Though the practice weapons were padded, and Bip had crammed as much of the training armor onto his body as possible, Rynford had still managed to beat him black and blue while demonstrating the finer points of "not being stabbed to death by something sharp." There had been some respite while Rynford had taken Bip through a few survival techniques, which mainly involved how to cook, wear, or otherwise recycle the animal you'd just killed. However, the relief had been short-lived, as the Huntmaster had decided to end the day by showing Bip some of the more interesting hand-to-hand combat techniques he had developed.

Bip had limped back to town in a daze, cold, wet, and exhausted beyond anything he had experienced in his life. Muscles that he had never known existed were aching ferociously, and his nose streamed a cold wave of snot. He curled up further still in his thick blankets and enjoyed the warmth and security of his bed. The ecstasy of relaxation was marred only by the looming realization that, at dawn the next day, the training would begin all over again.

7

Handen Strike Vs. The End of the World

Captain's log. *Day Two Hundred and Sixty Three.*

Progress continues as normal. I have to say, as temporary as I believed the arrangements would be, Kanick is appearing more and more like a home rather than an outpost. While many of the crew still brood for civilization, a few have begun to settle down and make the most of the situation…even come to enjoy it.

I must confess I reside in the latter camp.

Supplies are still plentiful for the time being. Various projects and committees to ensure a more comfortable existence in Kanick are currently being undertaken, and people are content to busy themselves cultivating our base into a more homely environment.

Though I have come to terms with our being stranded, I cannot help but feel guilty that there is currently not much we can do to further our original mission to protect Bersch. It seems wrong to settle down and relax while a planet is unwittingly heading toward catastrophe. All we can do is wait…

FINNEGUN LOOKED up from his wrist console as Handen approached. He took a brief moment to take in the scenery of Kanick, which still warmed him. The lush green village, surrounded by towering trees, was a far cry from the patch of lifeless snow they had originally crashed into. These days, life in Kanick was spent in individual housing rather than crammed together in barracks, and though Finnegun missed the camaraderie of those times, it was a relief to relax on the porch of his own private lodgings.

Handen stopped at the foot of Finnegun's porch and snapped a smart salute. Finnegun smiled briefly to himself. While the rest of the crew had grown relaxed and informal in their new community, Handen and his hunting party had retained the rigid military discipline of their station.

"At ease, Handen," said Finnegun, smiling wryly.

"Reporting from patrol, sir," said Handen.

"Ah, really? And how goes the hunting party?" said Finnegun.

"Excellent, sir. We've been pacifying the northern borders, sir. A large tribe of yetis had seen fit to take up residence by the heatshield, and so we dispersed them with a show of force. No casualties were sustained."

"Really? No casualties, eh? Hmm. Brilliant." Finnegun grinned nervously. The hunting party had flourished under Handen's strict and rigorous supervision, which had turned a group of men and women who previously would have had trouble with the concept of beating an egg into a team of skilled trackers, survivalists, and fighters. The hunting party had become close-knit, spending most of their time patrolling the Ice Plains and very little time in the security of the heatshield at all.

Though Finnegun understood the need for reconnaissance and security in the outlying regions of Kanick, he couldn't remember authorizing battle with a tribe of fifteen-foot monsters.

"These yetis," he said. "We couldn't have tried...reasoning with them?"

Handen's deadpan stare did not waver. "A messenger was sent to contact the yetis under a flag of negotiation, sir."

"And?"

"They ate the flag, sir, and tried to eat the messenger."

"Ah. So. No negotiations, then?"

"No, sir. They just tried to eat us, sir," said Handen. "You'd be surprised how many things out there want to eat us, sir," he concluded by way of explanation.

"Well," said Finnegun, at a loss for what to say. "Jolly good. Carry on, I suppose."

"Sir…" began Handen, and Finnegun bit his lip. This was a conversation he had seen coming for a long time.

When they had first landed on Bersch, Handen had been in his element, taking to crisis like a fish to water, but in the recent months, as the crew had settled down and the hunting party had reached an acceptable level of skill, Handen had become increasingly restless. Finnegun knew exactly what the Hostility Advisor was going to say.

"No, Handen," he said.

"Pardon, sir?" said Handen, feigning stupidity.

"You want to try to contact this planet's civilizations, Handen. Doubtless you have some dashingly intrepid quest in mind to save the world. Well, I'm sorry, but it's just impossible. We need you here."

"Julius, listen," Handen replied.

Finnegun stopped, stunned. That was the first time Handen had referred to him as anything other than "Sir" or "Captain."

Handen continued. "Things here are fine. The hunting party is taking care of itself. Kanick is more like a holiday camp than a survival outpost. I can't just sit here and wait for help. It's not in my nature."

Finnegun sighed. Handen was right, of course. The *Sentinel's* crew could ill afford to wait around and hope for the best. Not with the fate of the world at stake.

"What do you need?" he said, defeated.

"I've taken the liberty of drawing up a list of supplies. I'll also need the assistance of two of the more accomplished hunters."

"Done. Done. Take whatever you need. But who, may I ask, is going to be my Hostilities Advisor?"

"I thought Izzy was shaping up very nicely, sir."

Finnegun smiled. Thanks to Handen's hunting party, Izzy's

temperament had finally found an environment in which to flourish, and it had flourished abundantly, the buds of petty tantrum growing into a tactical understanding of violence that rivaled even Handen's.

"An excellent choice, I'm sure. When did you wish to leave?"

"Tomorrow, sir. At dawn."

"Dawn? Why dawn?"

Handen shrugged. "It's how we do things in the hunting party, sir."

AS THE FIRST light of day struck a cold dagger into the gray of the pre-dawn wilderness, Handen stared out into the slowly revealing horizons. The hunting party had escorted the three volunteers to the ice floes, which led out into the seemingly endless ocean.

Anchored to a fairly stable chunk of floating ice was a sea vessel constructed from leftover debris from the crash landing. The metal ship was powered by a series of small outboard motors that ran on a makeshift fuel the Elite-Gifted had managed to cultivate from local vegetation. Handen had no idea whether the vessel would be adequate for their journey, largely because he had no idea where their journey would take them. Though they had mapped Bersch extensively before entering chronostatic hibernation, quite a few millennia had passed since then, and all Handen was certain of was that the next continent was several hundred miles to the south.

They had decided to call the vessel the *Sentinel II*, purely for the sake of sentiment.

Handen turned to the hunting party. They stood solemnly in a row, their furs and weapons grayly silhouetted against the ever-white background. He would miss them. He would miss the wilderness.

Over the passing months, Handen had found he had an affinity with the Ice Plains. They offered him challenge and adventure, the two things he craved above all else. He had been annoyed when he had first taken on the hunting party, their whinging and complaining spoiling the soundless peace of the open tundra, their naivety and lack of respect taking the excitement from the danger. Eventually, though, through his personal training and the endless pressure of the wilds, the crew had turned into true hunters and had become one with the wilderness.

While the rest of the crew had struggled to build their homes and lives in the boundaries of Kanick, Handen and his comrades had found their place on the open run of the Ice Plains. Now they stood silently. There was little need for words in the hunting party, who could often communicate all they needed with a look or a hand gesture, but Handen felt there were a few things that needed to be said. He turned to Izzy, who held his gaze.

"I'm not needed here anymore," said Handen.

"Debatable," replied Izzy, her face as deadpan and unreadable as the former Hostility Advisor's.

"You'll do fine. You'll all do fine."

"I think so."

Handen surveyed the beckoning horizon again. He signaled for the two volunteers to prepare the boat for cast off. He turned back to Izzy and shook her hand, holding on a little longer than the formality of the gesture allowed for."It's a big, wide world out there," he said, an uncharacteristic half-smile breaking his face.

"Good luck," she said.

"You too. All of you."

The *Sentinel II* sailed into the brightening sea. Handen stood on the bow, looking back at the slowly shrinking shapes of the hunting party, his family, and his home willowing into a blurred nothing. Then he turned around, compelled by the seductive pull of new horizons. He smiled.

TWENTY-THREE MONTHS LATER, an honorary grave was dug for Handen and the volunteers.

KABLAAM!

Anyone standing next to the Dome would have been surprised by the deep, ominous rumble in the ground and the clouds of snow and ice that were shaken from the normally and reliably static building. Thankfully, the only thing near the outside of the Dome that could have been surprised was a cluster of penguins. The penguins, not being masters of environmental awareness, continued to shuffle around in the manner of creatures with not much else to do but shuffle.

KABLOOIE!!

Elders and councilmen walking around the upper levels of the Dome paused briefly as the ground wobbled beneath them, regained their balance and continued about their business as though nothing had happened. They were all aware of what had been scheduled in the lower levels for today and were quite used to the floor shaking and the thunderous—

KABLAMMY!!! sizzlesizzlesizzle...phhupt

Bip unblocked his ears and slowly opened his eyes. The practice room near the bowels of the Dome was gloomy and dark and thickly quiet, but Bip's vision swam with blue and purple flashes from the frantic light show that had seared across his glasses, and his ears rang with the reverberations of the almighty booms that had accompanied it. Where there had been five of the grinning test dummies at the end of the room, there now stood two, looking lonely next to three ominous piles of dust and rubble.

Up on the gantry, overlooking the vast and nearly empty practice room, Truggle coughed through the thick smoke from his pipe while Dunman cleaned the steam from his glasses.

"I think," said Truggle, slowly, "that Bip has seen enough of your commendable talent for exploding things, Glimton. Perhaps if you went over some theory now?"

Glimton looked up at the gantry, a slightly manic grin still skewing his thin features, his dark, round goggles reflecting a wicked glint from the lamps that shone down from the high ceiling. "Sorry, Truggle," he called, merrily. "Just demonstrating the finer points of rapid molecular discombobulation."

"Yes, well, as much as I enjoy watching you obliterate straw dummies, we are here for the purpose of developing Bip's knack and not your own," replied Truggle.

Glimton scratched his egg-like head and turned to regard Bip as if he had only just noticed he was there. Bip had changed a little over the past fortnight. Rynford's intense training sessions had left the volunteer looking tired and drawn, but already there was a slight set to his scrawny shoulders and a bit of a spring in his normal shuffle. Rynford's unorthodox fitness regimes still left Bip feeling like he wanted to die, but when he'd caught a look at himself in the mirror one evening before going to bed, he had been pleased to notice if not any *actual* muscle then at least the promise of muscular development on his normally unremarkable physique.

While Rynford insisted that Bip had a long way to go before he was ready for the wilderness, he had admitted that his rate of progress for the first two weeks was very nearly at a minimal level of acceptableness. With this sterling stamp of approval, Truggle had suggested that Bip pay more attention to developing his psyentific knack, and he had been turned over to the teachings of Glimton, who, despite his penchant for blowing things up and his legendary arrogance, was the most able psyentist in Kaneq.

Glimton adjusted the high collar of his white coat and peered at Bip through his shaded goggles.

"Well, well, well, well, well," he began. "Haven't we come a long way? It seems that Rynford has got you using all your muscles except the ones in your head!" He snickered a light and annoying snicker. Bip, who had learnt a great deal of interesting things under Rynford's supervision, albeit most of them involving the killing and processing of animals, opened his mouth to protest.

"No, no. Don't speak," interrupted Glimton. "I should imagine you don't have anything worthwhile to say, anyhow. I, after all, have shaken hands with the very fibers of being, have waltzed with the microscopic intricacies of life, have skipped the light fantastic and moved on to higher things, whereas you..." He looked Bip up and down. "You are a pleb."

Bip looked uncertainly up at the gantry where Truggle and Dunman sat. Truggle gave an apologetic shrug. Glimton continued to speak, his high-pitched and clipped tones echoing grandiosely around the practice room as he paced up and down.

"Oh, you may have been impressed by Rynford's flip-flops and what-nots, and you may think it's awfully clever to chuck sharpened pieces of wood at dumb beasts, but I..." Glimton turned his full attention back to Bip. "I will show you how to see what a flower is thinking, how to change the shape of stone, how to manipulate the very air you breathe!" Glimton was suddenly uncomfortably close to Bip, his voice a low murmur. "I will show you how to unlock your birthright!"

Bip leaned back slightly and blinked, his perplexed face reflected in the blackness of Glimton's goggles. "Good?" he said.

Glimton's manic smile collapsed instantly. He turned away and began muttering to himself. "Good? Good, he says? I offer him the secrets of the universe and he says 'good'? I ought to replace his eyeballs with his other balls just to teach him some respect! Ingrate! Unenthusiastic, disrespectful, little..." He spun wildly from his mutterings and raised his clawed hand to the gantry in spectacularly dramatic rage, his reedy voice now booming with fury. "You waste my time, Truggle! You give me this and call it a student? You waste my time!!"

There was an uncomfortable silence as the echoes died away.

"Anyhow," said Glimton, his demeanor changing from boiling rage to indifferent cheerfulness in a split-second, "I suppose we'd better get on with things. Busy, busy, busy, yes? The sands of time wait for no one, hmm? Let's talk a little theory, shall we?"

Bip reeled, unsure how to deal with the sudden shift in temperamental weather. He opted to shut up and listen as Glimton began talking animatedly about psyence, cheerfully preaching theory as if he hadn't just threatened to radically alter Bip's anatomy. He attempted to concentrate, but part of him couldn't help wishing he were out on patrol with Rynford, who was at least predictably insane.

"Where was I? Where was I?" muttered Glimton. "Ah, yes! Instructions! Everything is, at its core, a set of instructions! Little bits of information, a trillion billion invisible scraps of data, that tell a thing not only what it is but also what it does! A rock is a rock is a rock—but even a rock knows, on some infinitesimally small level, that it *is* a *rock*! Do you understand!?"

Bip was uncomfortably aware that Glimton seemed to be getting over excited and wisely chose not to say anything. Instead, he smiled and nodded politely.

"Grins like an idiot," Glimton said scornfully, before continuing his lecture as though he had never interrupted himself. "So even the smallest and dullest of things are aware, on a level too far below what we understand as comprehension to recognize without looking very closely indeed, not just of what they are, but what they do! A rock knows to lie still and be hard! It's what it does! If it didn't, it would be a pretty useless rock, wouldn't you say? Ahahahaha!!"

Bip deemed it appropriate to give a polite chuckle. He also stepped back a little bit.

"Laughs like a girl," Glimton muttered angrily, before once again launching into his rant. "Instructions! The important thing to remember is that on the most microscopically microscopic of levels, all these instructions are written on the same paper! The same energy! They can all be beheld, and if understood, they can be persuaded to change! That is the process of the Knack, the secret of the Psyence, the legacy of our Ancestors! A rock is a rock is a rock—but it used to be magma, maybe, or sand, or part of a mountain, or even a star! Even the lowliest of pebbles, at its core, knows how to be a mountain! The smallest of seeds can dream of the towering oak! And these dreams can be seen in the instruction, can be read, can be understood—and can be altered!"

Bip stood and listened attentively. It was a vague and introductory lecture on the nature of the knack, usually reserved for children many years his junior, but he couldn't help but be awed by Glimton's passion and enthusiasm.

"Stands there listening like a...like a...like a *pleb*!" shouted Glimton, for no good reason. Then, so suddenly that Bip fell over, he blew up one of the few remaining test dummies. The dummy, writhing briefly under Glimton's outstretched finger, expanded radically before igniting into a ball of flame, showering flaming straw and cloth, its grinning head rocketing into the air and navigating a gentle arc before coming to rest between Bip's legs.

"Meep!" said Bip, too horrified to say anything useful.

"You see!?" screamed Glimton. "The Dummy already knows how to be a lots of different pieces, it remembers being molecular! It was just a matter of reminding it! With a vengeance!!!"

When the echoes died away, a polite coughing from the gantry broke the uncomfortable silence that always surrounds the unpredictably explosive.

"Glimton," said Truggle soothingly. "I believe you're getting a bit carried away again, yes?"

"Ahahahahaha," said Glimton. "Silly me. How embarrassing. So sorry. Very sorry." Glimton picked up the head of the straw dummy and addressed it.

"Are we sorry, Mr. Head?" said Glimton, and then, in quite a convincing act of ventriloquism, replied, "We certainly are, Mr. Glimton—we're very sorry!"

"Yes, that's right, Mr. Head! Very sorry indeed!"

"Boy howdy!"

"Ahahahaha!"

"Please don't hurt me, Mr. Glimton! I won't tell your secrets!"

"Silence, you ignorant troll!!" screamed Glimton, and obliterated Mr. Head in a wave of fire.

Bip, Dunman, and Truggle all stood with their mouths open in idiot disbelief—whether at the fate of Mr. Head or the continually revealing depths of Glimton's humongous eccentricities, no one could tell.

Glimton turned to face the gantry, the mask of psychotic rage ebbing from his features.

"And so ends today's lesson," he said. "Tomorrow we shall discuss the Persuasion of Physics, the Cajoling of Base Substances and the

Exploding of Things I Have Lying Around. Good day." He turned and walked calmly out of the practice room.

Bip, in his utter confusion and terror, applauded nervously.

LATER, Bip sat with Truggle in the Empty Goat, a cup of hot, sweet tea clutched in his thin fingers.

"I know he's a little bit…odd," began Truggle.

"A little!?" cried Bip. "He's off his rocker, is what he is!"

"Well…yes," Truggle conceded. "But he's also the finest psyentific mind in the community."

Bip gulped his tea. "So you keep saying, but so far all I've learned is that a madman with the ability to explode things with his mind is not good company. And I'm pretty sure I already knew that, so I haven't really learned anything!"

"Nevertheless," sighed Truggle, "Glimton is the best chance we have of preparing your knack for the outside world, where I'm fairly sure that exploding straw dummies will be the least of your worries."

Bip shivered. He was beginning to have serious doubts about saving the world.

SEA SPRAYED over the prow of the *Sentinel II* as it ploughed effortlessly through the choppy ocean, its metal frame gleaming a brilliant orange in the setting sun, its sharp symmetry slicing smoothly through the oncoming waves. Over the rushing wind and the roar of the ocean, the sound of the ship's outboard motors could be heard burring steadily and confidently.

Handen was pleased. They had sailed for eight days straight without a single sign of bad weather or any other impediments. Supplies and fuel were still plentiful, and the *Sentinel II* was as in as good a condition as she had been when she had first been put together. Widge and Beggs, the two hunter volunteers, busied themselves checking over the engine stats and the short-range scanner they had managed to salvage from the original *Sentinel*. Their bustle was fruitless, though, as there had not been an inkling of incident since the ship had cast off.

Beggs yawned, ruffled her short, feathered hair, and relaxed a little in her console chair. Widge, however, maintained an iron vigil over his scanner display. Handen surveyed the reassuringly boring horizon through his view panel. It looked like smooth sailing all the way.

"Um…sir?" said Widge, not taking his eyes from the scanner.

Handen closed his eyes. He knew that any question that began with "um" was likely to be trouble. "What is it, Mr. Widge?" he said.

"There's something coming up on the short-range, sir—something big. I think it might be land."

"Land? Impossible, I would have…" Handen stopped. He looked out of his view panel again. What before had been an idyllic image of clear seas had now turned gray and murky. A thick fog had sprung from seemingly nowhere.

"Cut the engines," ordered Handen, and for the first time since the beginning of their journey, the hum of the outboard motors ceased.

The three sailors stiffened slightly. It was eerily quiet, and not just because of the lack of engine noise. There was no wind and no slap of waves. The *Sentinel II* didn't even rock slightly in the water.

"The scanner is still reading a large mass, sir. It has to be land—it's too big to be anything else."

Unease crept down Handen's spine like the fingers of some swamp-dwelling thing. "Widge, take the controls. Beggs, accompany me up on deck. Let's take a look around."

Before leaving the control bridge, Handen unthinkingly picked up some choice weapons and secured them about his person, adding a short sword, and a long bullwhip to the spear and dagger combination he usually preferred. The decision to pick up his weapons was a nearly unconscious act, a nervous habit rather than a planned defense.

Up on the deck, the thick, yellowish fog obscured any long-range view, making it difficult to tell if they were, indeed, approaching land.

It also seemed to toy with the acoustics of the sailor's voices, making them seem hollow and distant.

"Look over here, sir," said Beggs, who had for some reason begun talking in a low whisper.

Handen looked over the ship's bow where Beggs had pointed and could not help but stare. The ocean was dead still, barely rippling as it came into contact with the *Sentinel II*. The water, as far as Handen could make out, was as dark and smooth as some black mirror, or a slab of onyx. Handen shivered, not sure whether it was merely the cold air that chilled him, though the thick fog let through no sea breeze.

"Land ho, sir!" cried the voice of Widge from the control bridge. Handen looked around wildly and saw that Widge was right. Through the thick fog, he could see the silhouette of what looked like a small island. All of a sudden, a low, rumbling moan seemed to saturate the surroundings, bellowing like the bending of iron or the ghosts of a thousand whales. Handen shivered again, first suspecting they had hit rock, then realizing that the *Sentinel II* still had not moved. The low moan sounded again, and the glass-still waters of the ocean began to ripple into steady, rhythmic waves. The island silhouette seemed to be getting closer, or bigger, and the low moan sounded again, louder this time. As it did, the seawater around them began to bubble, and the rhythm of the waves began to intensify. Clouds began to blacken the sky, and rain and thunder quickly joined the stormy chorus. There was a sound like a giant waterfall coming from the direction of the island.

Realization dawned a brand new day of terror in Haden's guts. "Start the engines," he muttered.

"Sir?"

"*Start the damn engines!*"

Before Widge could react, Handen's worst fears were confirmed—the silhouette *had* been getting closer and was also getting bigger. As the fog cleared and the sea began to boil madly, a colossal black fin was revealed, already towering above the boat, water cascading from it as it rose steadily through the fog.

"Incredible..." murmured Handen. Everything began to take on a dreamlike quality now that an intense fear paralyzed his senses and dulled his consciousness. Beside him, Beggs began to scream hoarsely.

The fin continued to rise, the resulting waves sending the *Sentinel II* sprawling backward. As the fin rose, the water around them seemed to darken still further, until the shoulders and head of some terrible force of nature arose from the depths. For a brief and giddying moment, Handen stared into an eye the size and color of a full moon. As water rained around him in a torrent and the vessel rocked manically, Handen stood face to face with a Kraken.

The incredible beast's head looked something like the skull of a dead fish, though a grimy, burnt black rather than white. Its huge, pupil-less eyes bulged over a mouth full of a thousand teeth like giant needles. From its cavernous throat, an ear-piercing screech shattered the gloom like a million fingers on glass. And still it continued to rise.

Handen stood stock still, frozen with a terror he had never experienced before, while beside him, Beggs was blue in the face from screaming.

Widge, with the slight illusion of safety the control deck offered him, recovered from his terror far more quickly than his comrades and prepared to initiate the vessel's weaponry. Though the *Sentinel II* had been built solely for exploration, it had still been constructed by hunters, and hunters especially knew the value of a good weapon to the explorer. Thus, at the prow of the ship, four heavy harpoon cannons stood poised and ready—though even Widge, through a cloud of panic, knew they wouldn't do much good against a target the size of the Kraken. Still, he punched the firing keys for all four harpoons and watched as the powerful cannons unleashed their payload into the neck of the rising leviathan.

Despite the size of the towering sea-creature, the harpoons, by a twist of chance, managed to hit the Kraken in one of its few weak areas. The beast reared up in pain, causing an enormous wave to wash over the hapless *Sentinel II,* slamming Handen and Beggs to the rear of the ship. The shock snapped Handen out of his terror trance.

"Start the engines! Start the engines!" he screamed, his voice barely audible over the angry screeches of the Kraken. Luckily, the same thought had occurred to Widge at the same time, and he quickly punched in the ignition sequence. The engines roared into life and began to move the *Sentinel II* away from the raging sea-monster. However, compared to their goliath adversary, the progress of the vessel seemed far too slow.

As the beast reared up to its full height, water cascading from its shoulders like so many rivers, Handen was surprised to see a smooth, human-like torso eclipse the setting sun, and even more surprised to see two scaly, finned, and heavily clawed arms rise to its throat and begin scratching the harpoons away from its gills. Seeing that the beast would soon recover from their meager assault, Handen knew that there was no way they could outrun the giant reach of a Kraken.

At this point, Beggs, whose survival instincts had finally surpassed her terror, prepared to equate an attack. Beggs had been Elite-Gifted before joining the hunting party and knew a wide range of aggressive equations. Screaming hysterically all the time, she began launching torrents of lightning at the chest of the sky-scraping horror. Handen watched as the Kraken screamed with rage, swatting at the energy bolts as they exploded about its torso. Beggs, her face contorted with a bizarre mix of terror and rage, looked almost a match for the titan as sparks crackled from her fingers and hair and her clothes flapped crazily in her own personal energy storm. Handen wished he could contribute somehow to their escape but knew, deep down, that even if he had had double the equating power of Beggs, they still would not be able to slow the beast sufficiently.

The Kraken, recovering from Beggs's onslaught, lifted a planet-like fist high into the sky and swung it down toward the *Sentinel II*. Beggs stopped her assault and looked up in dumb horror as the leviathan's fist plummeted toward them like a meteor strike.

Well that's it then, thought Handen's head as the world slowly began to eclipse. *We're dead.*

Bugger that, said his legs, and propelled the rest of him over the side of the ship. He began to swim madly for freedom as the Kraken's fist crashed into the *Sentinel II* behind him, obliterating it totally and sending out a tidal wave that rippled hugely from the point of impact. Handen held his breath and closed his eyes as he was lifted by the swell of the humongous wave. He had expected to be dragged under but, by a million to one chance, the wave lifted him to its peak, carrying him far from the reach of the Kraken. He flew through the air as the wave broke, narrowly missing hunks of burning wreckage from the *Sentinel II*, zipping and ripping in all directions, then was dumped unceremoniously into the brine.

Handen erupted from the choppy waters with a panicky splutter and was briefly tempted to sigh with relief but quickly realized the inappropriateness of such an action. He was far from out of danger yet. The Kraken, its opponent vanquished, dived back down to the deeper waters it had emerged from, letting out a victorious shriek as waves exploded around it. The undertow from the retreating monster began sucking down the floating debris—and Handen along with it.

Great, Handen had time to think, *so I miraculously avoid being crushed only to be drowned instead...*

However, a part of Handen much less cynical than his brain, which had kept him alive in situations where lesser men would have perished, began to search for a way out of this new predicament. As the tail of the Kraken submerged in the distance and Handen felt himself being pulled unstoppably downward, he happened to catch a glimpse of something that almost made him laugh out loud. Only a few feet away, circling endlessly amongst other miscellaneous debris from the *Sentinel II*, was a fragment of the ship that contained one of the outboard motors, running aimlessly at full power.

Handen briefly applauded the decision to make the vessel's motors independent of one another in case they had to lighten their load or construct a new vessel. Or, apparently, in case the ship was obliterated by an angry sea-monster. He was torn away from his self-congratulation by the rapid pull of the ocean beneath him.

The motor, burring only a few meters away, might as well have been on the other side of the world for all the progress Handen could make against the deadly undertow. He had one idea left, and it would be a one-shot, hit-or-miss action that would either save his life or merely accelerate his demise. Handen stopped struggling enough to reach for his bullwhip and, with a skillful flick of his wrist and a mighty crack, managed to snag the sturdy whip around the motor. He sagged with relief as he felt himself being pulled away from the sucking undercurrent and watched with fatigued interest as the unpowered debris was slowly pulled under. He spared a thought for Widge and Beggs, his most trusted allies, and for the *Sentinel II*, which had suffered a fate worse than that of its predecessor.

Sighing heavily, he managed to secure the bullwhip around his shoulders. Then, with the tow of the motor keeping his head above water and the still-fresh horror swimming in his mind, he passed out in a dead faint.

8

Interlude—Even Gods Need Someone to Complain to...

He was the spirit of the planet of Bersch. He was the sigh in the wind. He was the glint in the stream. He was known by a thousand names and faces: The Almighty, Krund, Great Heebie Jeebie, Torrac, and in one unusual religious case, he was even known as Molly From Next Door. Mostly, he was referred to as God, as that was not just his nature but also his job description.

Currently he was putting his feet up in a sunny, beautifully kept garden and having a natter with his old friend Ted.

God had chosen to adopt one of his more common appearances, that of an old man dressed in a white robe, with a long, flowing beard. He preferred this incarnation. There was something fundamentally relaxing about being an old man in a white robe. He took a long sip of his tea and began complaining again.

"It's not enough that grass continues to grow and that rivers continue to flow. They want bright lights and visions! Party tricks!" He spat the word "visions." "Pah! Since when was seeing believing? People only see what they want to see! And even if they did see me, they'd probably only be disappointed."

Ted nodded sympathetically, pushing his flat cap back on his head.

"It's the age of reason, I'm afraid. I've seen it before. It tends to get people confused a little," he said.

God tutted. "Age of reason, indeed. People would be a lot happier if they just stopped poking around in things and got on with their lives. Do you know I overheard some schmuck the other day saying that, if I truly existed, then why would I allow bad things to happen?"

Ted nodded again. He had heard that one a lot from other Gods.

God continued. "Oh, I could have given him such a slap! But it's the same with the other types as well. Something wonderful happens, 'Oh! 'Tis the will of God!' Something terrible happens and it's, 'Oh! 'Tis the will of God!' Honestly, sometimes I feel like just grabbing them and saying, 'Listen, you punk, if an earthquake happens, it's because of necessary environmental pressures, and if you find a fiver on the floor, it's because someone dropped it!'"

Ted nodded sympathetically and sipped at his tea. He was used to Gods getting a bit wound up. It's hard when everyone blames you for everything.

"I mean, you know me, Ted—I get on with things, I make sure things are happening like they're supposed to. Don't these people know how difficult evapotranspiration is? I don't have time for all this theological argumentative rubbish. We have a very nice set-up here on Bersch, and people should really just make the most of it and stop giving me hassle every time they hit their thumb with a hammer or whatever."

Ted nodded. He was glad to lend an ear whenever God was feeling a little irate, but there were more important things to talk about at present.

"You wanted to talk about the upcoming destruction of Bersch?" he said, politely cutting short God's rant.

"Oh, yes." God gave an embarrassed chuckle. "I do go on sometimes, don't I?"

Ted waved a hand dismissively and poured God another cup of tea.

"Yes, where was I?" said God. "The Massive Ball of Death. I've tried some subtle warnings about it—you know, appearing in dreams and such—but mostly people just ignore it."

"The age of reason," laughed Ted.

"Don't get me started again!" God chuckled. "Anyway. I'm not sure that, even if the whole world was fully aware of the approaching disaster, they could do anything to stop it. I don't think they have the power. As you know, this is a little out of my jurisdiction, so…er…do you have anything in the cards?"

Ted carefully put down his teacup. "All I can say is that forces are in play, and right now things could go either way. This universe, we know, operates solely on the perceptions of Order and Chaos, and the balance therein. All I can tell you is that it's all a bit up in the air at the minute. It's fifty-fifty."

"And the Caretakers?" said God.

"They're doing their best, but the Discordance have given them a bit of a low blow this time. They're fighting dirtier than usual."

"I see. That's a pity," said God solemnly.

"Cheer up, God," said Ted. "If the worst comes to the worst, at least you won't have to worry about philosophers any more, will you?"

9

Bip Plunkerton Vs. The End of
the World

Huddled in the unceasing blizzard of the Ice Plains, the wild snowcow grazed dumbly on the thistle-like shrubs that grew sporadically across the wilderness. In comparison to the domesticated Kaneqian snowcow, the wild snowcow was leaner, had more prominent horns, and was often much angrier. This was probably because it didn't get regular haircuts and more often than not couldn't see very well.

The temper of this specific snowcow was particularly nasty, which was why it had strayed from the rest of its herd to dine by itself. In fact, the temper of this snowcow was so particularly nasty that when Bip—who had been sneaking up on it for some time—prodded it in the jacksy with a spear, it flew into a near-incoherent rage.

The snowcow whirled around and came face-to-face with Bip, whose terrified and apologetic grin did nothing to quell its nuclear irritation. Huffing a great cloud of steam from its nostrils, the snowcow charged.

Bip legged it, a constant litany of "Dammit, dammit, dammit, dammit!" giving rhythm to his breathing.

It had been his turn to get breakfast that morning, and the solitary snowcow, even though it dwarfed Bip by a good two feet, had seemed the most likely target. Running in his panic, though, pursued by several hundred pounds of sharpened bovine, Bip was beginning to have doubts about his choice.

Unexpectedly, Bip stood his ground and whirled around to face the onrush of the snowcow. The beast lowered its head, readying it horns for a swift and brutal impaling. At the last possible second, Bip rolled to his left. The charging cow missed him by inches. Momentarily confused by the absence of gore on its horns, it tried to brake and turn at the same time in a flurry of hoof and horn. In its fury, it had failed to notice that Bip had been standing only a few feet in front of a vertical cliff face. The great beast scrambled briefly before falling to its doom with a mournful "Mooooo!"

Bip stood panting, his heart hammering a crazy tattoo against his ribs.

"Well done, lad!" came the voice of Rynford from a safe observation point. "Now get that mess cleaned up and let's see what we can stick on the grill!"

<hr>

"THAT WAS a novel way of taking care of the snowcow, son. Personally, I would have just beaten it to death with a club, but each to his own, I suppose."

Rynford raised a chunk of roasted beef to his mouth and chomped hungrily. Fortunately, the impact of the snowcow at the bottom of the cliff had meant that Bip had to do very little to prepare the meat for eating. It was more a case of picking up the bite-sized bits.

They were eating in the shelter of their usual breakfast cave. Bip reflected that he had begun to enjoy these moments. Despite the daily terror, hardship, and flirtation with certain death, he had developed a sense of camaraderie with Rynford that he had come to anticipate and enjoy. The old Huntmaster had become something of a father figure to him. Or at least a crazy uncle figure. He often wished he could say the same about Glimton, who still hadn't ceased to shock and awe the young trainee with his unpredictable temper tantrums. These mood swings had not improved when, despite Glimton's constant scream-ing, Bip had failed to make any real progress with his psyentific knack. Bip remembered his last lesson, when Glimton, in an unchar-acteristically calm mood, had tried to show him the benefits of medi-tating. They had sat cross-legged on the practice room floor, attempting to equate the Fire Dance, a basic exercise in molecular control.

"The Fire Dance is simple in its equating. Firstly, you have to visu-alize the components of your target. You must visualize the air mole-cules in front of you. See them swaying and colliding. See them dance," Glimton had said. Bip had attempted to visualize.

"And now that we can see them, we can make contact with their energy, we can communicate, we can see the equation. Now all we have to do is persuade the molecules to increase the tempo of the dance. Get them to jig. Faster and faster." Bip had concentrated, visu-alized the air molecules tap-dancing into a frenzy.

"As they dance," Glimton had continued, "they get warm. Now we have to encourage that heat, encourage the fire." Tiny sparks began to interlace and sway before Glimton's eyes. Then, with a soothing gentleness, a wave of fire had rippled softly in front of him, swaying with the currents of the air. "Visualize it, Bip. Make them dance." Bip had concentrated...

Concentrated...

Concentrated...

With a sound like a wet burp, a small puff of flame had appeared in front of Bip and landed in his crotch. He'd had no trouble visualizing dancing after that, as he hopped erratically around the room, his screams of panic mixing with Glimton's hysterical and merciless laughter...

"You all right there, lad?" said Rynford, shaking Bip from his gloomy thoughts. "You zoned out on me there for a bit."

"Sorry, Rynford. Just thinking is all."

"About the psyence thing again?"

"Yeah," said Bip glumly.

"I wouldn't worry about it too much, laddie. There've been plenty of volunteers who have ventured out with little or no knack. Fair enough, none of them have been seen again, but then again, none of the volunteers have been seen again anyway, so..." Rynford stopped when he saw the appalled look on Bip's face. "Er...sorry, lad. Not the most encouraging of words, I know. I tell you what." Rynford reached into one of his many satchels and pulled out something wrapped in oiled leather. "I was saving this for when you left, but you may as well have it now."

Bip unwrapped the leather and gasped appreciatively at what he saw inside. It was a Kaneqian sidesword. It was roughly two feet in length, with a delicately thin and wickedly sharp double-sided blade coming to a slight curve at the end. The workmanship on this particular blade was exquisite, with patterns of thorns embroidered all the way from the tip of the blade to the guard.

"Don't be put off by the girly designs," muttered Rynford, embarrassed. "They actually help the blood run off the blade."

Bip nodded and continued his examination of the sword. Kaneqians very rarely used swords, spears being more than adequate for their uncommon instances of combat, but the sidesword seemed perfect for Bip—light, manageable, and deadly even in the hands of an amateur. He stood and made a few experimental slashes with the sword. It made a pleasant swishing sound.

"I was going to give it to my son, if I ever had one," Rynford continued. "You know, just until he was old enough to carry a real weapon."

"It's brilliant, Rynford. Thanks. What's it called?"

"Called?" Rynford frowned. "It's called a sword, you bloody eejit."

"No, I mean, don't people usually give swords a name?"

"Fair enough. Um...I'll call this sword...Brian."

"Brian?" questioned Bip.

"Brian." Rynford nodded.

"Why Brian?"

"I dunno. Just always liked the sound of it. Nothing wrong with Brian," Rynford huffed defensively.

"No, no! Brian's fine. Very...serious sounding. I suppose."

He swished the sword through the air again, getting to grips with the restrictions of the hand guard and the balance of the blade.

"It's great."

"Well, I know you're not much good with a spear, so I thought maybe you'd get on better with this. I'll give you a few practice spars with it and see how you get on. After all, you're leaving soon. Can't go into the wide world without a weapon you feel comfortable with."

Bip nodded, suddenly knowing that he was going to miss Rynford terribly when he left. Of all of his few friends, even Michaelmas, Rynford had shared something unique and special with Bip. He had taught him to avoid being killed in nasty ways, and that warranted affection of a sort.

"But remember, lad," Rynford continued, "cunning, skill, ingenuity; these are our weapons! These are our teeth!"

BIP LAY AWAKE. It was his last evening before he set off into the unknown. He had spent the morning and afternoon with his mother and Michaelmas, neither of whom had said very much, but had sat gloomily, occasionally squeezing Bip's hand or telling him how proud they were. He had spent the evening with Bailey and his few friends, who still had no idea he was going, and had enjoyed a final drink in the Empty Goat. Bailey had been a little puzzled at Bip's goodbye, which had been a bit more emotional than even their level of drunkenness had called for.

It had been hard for Bip not to tell his friends what he was doing. It had been hard for him not to tell anyone. He had felt like standing on his roof and shouting into the night, "See you later, then. I'm off to save the world now. Don't wait up." But, of course, he couldn't. He could only disappear like a snowman in a blizzard, probably never to return. He had cried a little, he wasn't ashamed to say. He would miss his mother and Michaelmas and his friends. He would miss Truggle and Rynford, and even, to a certain extent, he would miss Glimton. Most of all, he would miss his trouble-free, simple Kaneqian existence, which until a few months ago had seemed like the whole world.

He didn't feel ready, of course. He wasn't sure that anyone could feel truly ready for the task ahead of him. His final assessments hadn't helped his confidence much either, with Rynford grudgingly admitting that Bip had reached an adequate level of survival skill, and Glimton refusing to admit that Bip had even an ounce of psyentific talent. Truggle had remained firm, though, insisting with an inexplicable confidence that Bip would more than shape up to the task in hand.

Truggle. He would miss Truggle. The strange old man he had always thought no more than a harmless, loony old duffer had turned out to be a keeper of fantastic secrets and terrible knowledge. Bip couldn't quite explain it, but ever since he'd first looked through those goggles and seen the true origins of Kaneq, he had felt like he had always known. Always known that the Dome, was, in fact, the long-beached vessel of his distant ancestors on the *Sentinel*. Always known that Kaneq had a deeper purpose. Truggle had called it genetic memory, though Bip preferred to think of it as spiritual inheritance, which while admittedly sounding a bit nebulous, was a little more warm and personal than Truggle's terminology.

Truggle. He'd had a final talk with Truggle about his upcoming journey. They had talked about the Clarions and their purpose, and the universal struggle between Order and Chaos. Then Truggle had talked about something called the Discordance, a race of beings that had devoted its allegiance to Chaos, with powers, Truggle had hinted, exceeding those of the Clarions.

"Deception," he had said. "Cunning, half-truths, and lies. Bad influence. These are the weapons of the Discordance. Be careful of those who would try to sap your will—these are the agents of adverse randomicity."

Finally, Truggle had taken him deep into the sublevels of the Dome, where in an unremarkable room at the end of an unremarkable corridor stood a huge iron obelisk. On it, stretching high toward the ceiling, were the names of every volunteer and the year they had left in. All the way from a chap named Handen, in year two, to the name of his father, in year nine hundred and eighty six. Bip's name, for better or worse, would be the final name added to the obelisk.

Bip had broken down. Standing before the weight of the massive obelisk, he felt a huge physical pressure on his shoulders and sank to his knees. The responsibility of taking on the mantle of a volunteer seemed too great. Truggle had left him for a while, to deal with his emotions.

Tomorrow, at dawn, his quest would begin. He would face unknown adversaries and unknown odds to warn a civilization he had never met that its doom was at hand.

He was more than a little nervous.

HANDEN STRIKE AWOKE and instantly began spluttering the lungful of seawater that clogged his throat. He retched for a while onto the rock he had been clinging to, then looked around. He was wedged in between two jagged rocks that seemed to appear from nowhere in the middle of the ocean. Farther down he could hear the splutter of the motor he was still attached to. He turned in the direction of the sound and saw the motor struggling weakly against another rock until, with a few defiant coughs, it died utterly, and the battered piece of debris it was attached to begin to sink. Even in his half-concussed confusion, Handen's almost automatic survival instincts gave him the presence of mind to unwrap the bullwhip from his shoulders. He watched helplessly as it disappeared under the waves with the rest of the debris.

Still dizzy from confusion and half drowned from...well, water, Handen began to take in his surroundings. The sun was beating pleasantly on his head as a steady rhythmic wave rocked him up and down. He heard the distant cry of what sounded like a seagull. Realizing the implications, Handen scrambled his way up onto the rock he had been clinging to and stood on top.

Not too far away—not very far away at all—was a comfortable-looking shoreline. Handen laughed triumphantly, or at least tried to, but he was interrupted by a coughing fit as he dislodged more of the ocean from his belly.

Land! He had made it to land! And land meant civilization! His mission was nearing its final stages. Handen took hold of his excitement and began to assess the situation at hand. There would be time for celebration later. Right now, in his exhausted state, weaponless and armor-less, he would have to swim to shore and find fresh water and food and see to the various nagging injuries he had sustained during the incident with the Kraken. After that, he would have to find out just where the hell he was. Still, Handen's spirits had lifted considerably. He felt as if he was almost at the finish line.

BIP STOOD at the heatshield exit, preparing himself for the first few steps that would take him ever farther away from his homeland. He secured the fastening on his insulating leathers and oilskin and checked the strap on his huge, overladen backpack. On his head was the traditional Kaneqian travel-hat, a wide brimmed canvas affair studded with various pockets and pouches. It resembled a rucksack with a brim and chinstrap.

His peers crowded around him, waiting to wish him well on his quest. The only person who knew that he was leaving but hadn't shown up was Bip's mother. They had exchanged a solemn and sad goodbye earlier in the morning over a breakfast hearty enough for ten people.

Michaelmas approached and put a meaty hand on Bip's shoulder.

"I'm gonna miss you, mate, no lie. 'Twont be the same without you."

"I'll miss you too, Michaelmas. You've always looked out for me."

"Aye lad, aye. And I always will, long as I'm able. I know it'll be cold out there, so I brought you a little something to keep out the chill." Michaelmas reached into his apron and pulled out two large bottles of something golden-brown. Bip saw the label and gulped. Michaelmas had brought two bottles of Mr. Braindead's Very Special Infamous

Goose, the most lethal alcohol concoction in Kaneq. It certainly would keep the chill out. In fact, it would likely set his head on fire if he drank it straight.

"Cheers, Michaelmas," he said, and stowed the bottles in one of his many pouches.

"Well, as long as we're giving presents," interrupted the reedy voice of Glimton, "you may as well have these." The psyentist poured several acorns into Bip's outstretched hands.

Bip tried not to look nonplussed. "Thanks, Glimton. Acorns. Just what I needed."

"Don't patronize me, you idiot! I spent a lot of time and effort reprogramming those acorns. Just add water and wait and they'll grow into something useful."

Bip peered at one of the acorns. The word "BOAT" was carved into it in copperplate writing.

"Wow," said Bip, genuinely impressed. "Thanks. Thanks a lot."

"Don't thank me, you numbskull. Truggle made me give them to you." With that, Glimton turned his back and stormed off, pausing only to turn around and shout, "Good luck, by the way, you talentless pleb!"

Bip couldn't help but smile.

Next it was Rynford's turn to approach. He clasped Bip's hand in a beefy handshake.

"I guess we've already said all we have to say. I've got no more to give you other than Brian there."

"You've given me a lot more than just the sword, Rynford." Bip grinned. "Thanks to you, I think I might just stand a chance out there."

"Well, don't get your hopes up, laddie." Rynford laughed. "Seriously, though, I wish I'd had more time to train you."

"Me too. I enjoyed it. It was tiring, nightmarish, soul-destroying work, but I don't think I'll ever taste anything quite as good as your driftdigger steak."

Rynford smiled. "Remember, lad, eat them before they can eat you."

Bip nodded and made his way to the heatshield exit point. Truggle rowed his way up to meet him as the psyentists opened the exit. A bitter wind rolled from the Ice Plains almost immediately, causing Bip to wince slightly.

"This is it, young Bip," said Truggle. "Do you think you're ready?"

Bip's brow creased in honest consideration. "No," he replied.

Truggle laughed out loud. "Have a little faith, Bip. I think we'll be seeing you again, you know." And once again Truggle's eyes flashed with that sharp intelligence Bip had seen on the first day they had spoken.

Bip said nothing. He took one last look at his friends, adjusted his glasses, waved, and walked out into the wilderness.

HANDEN SPLUTTERED and staggered his way onto the shoreline. He had not anticipated how weak his recent ordeals had made him, and the swim from the rocky outcrop had very nearly finished him off. He looked around desperately for a sign of life on the suddenly barren-looking shoreline. He had been hoping for a fishing community, or any sign of a population, but he could neither hear nor see anything that might have attested to this. He was in bad need of rest, but a pressing thirst and hunger told him that lying down might not be such a good idea. He had a feeling he'd have trouble getting up again.

He surveyed the horizons of this new land. Not too far away, a tree line began—and trees suggested a possibility of water. After the tree line, however, things did not look so good. A huge and jagged range of flat-headed mountains cut across his vision, stretching to the left and right as far as he could see. Given what appeared to be a lack of civilization anywhere on the right side of the mountains (e.g., Handen's side of the mountains) it was dawning on him that in order to continue his search, he'd have to scale them.

Handen gritted his teeth. Hungry, thirsty, and exhausted beyond reasonable endurance, he set his stone-like jaw and made his way to the tree line. He had faced many a challenge in his time and would be damned if he'd give in to despair now just because of a few upstart mountains. He strode determinedly across the sand, bending down to pick up a piece of driftwood with appropriate clubbing potential. It made him feel a little better.

BIP TRUDGED DETERMINEDLY through the thick snow, Kaneq having long since disappeared over the horizon. He couldn't even see the haze of the heatshield anymore. He was making his way toward the ice floes, which would then lead him to the ocean. This, he had been told, would be the quickest way to reach the next continent, which was the closest likelihood of a civilized society. It would mean sailing, something that very few Kaneqians were particularly adept at, but Glimton assured him that his acorn "BOAT" would be able to take care of itself.

The ice floes were a long journey by foot, but Bip knew the way and was fairly sure he would make it in good time. Despite leaving his lifelong home, Bip was feeling strangely optimistic, almost excited. The words of his friends still echoed warmly in his ears and gave him a smug sort of confidence.

By golly, I'll save this planet or my name ain't Bip Plunkerton, he thought to himself, and couldn't help laughing out loud.

It was a premature laugh, though, as Bip quickly realized when a mound of snow that had appeared just the same as any other mound of snow suddenly exploded before him, revealing a fifteen-foot monster of white hair and yellow fang. The beast uttered a bone-shaking bellow and Bip, despite his month-long intensive training, took one look at the roaring monstrosity and fainted in utter terror.

BIP AWOKE IN A WARM PLACE. *I must still be in bed,* he thought. *Yet to leave. All that huge bellowing monster thing must have been a dream. Better yet, maybe that entire volunteer thing was a dream. Maybe I'll wake up and it'll be before the Apprentice Fair and the planet won't be going to explode and Truggle will still be an old fool who can barely string a sentence together. Keeper of the Ancient Wisdom, indeed!* It seemed wonderfully preposterous now that he thought about it.

Then he realized he was wet as well as warm. *It's possible you fell asleep in the bath, surely?* his brain yelled desperately. *Whatever you do, don't open your eyes! Just pretend you fell asleep in the bath—the alternative's too horrible to contemplate. Trust me—I'm your brain!*

With a sense of growing horror, Bip, despite his unconsciousness's best efforts to protect him, opened his eyes. He was in a pot. A pot filled with warm water. Warm water, he knew, that was gradually going to get hotter.

He looked frantically around his surroundings. He was in a bright cave—more of a room carved out of snow than a natural rock formation—and he was sitting in a large iron pot with a few thistles and root vegetables floating around him. Under the pot burned a small but determined fire. He had been stripped of his gear and clothes, and on one of the cave walls a large selection of poorly made but incredibly sharp-looking carving knives hung with an easy kind of promise.

Bip gulped, remembering the yeti that had ambushed him. Yetis were an intelligent sort of creature in their own way, capable of tool use and communication (and cuisine cookery, apparently, thought a treacherous part of Bip's subconscious), but their intelligence was tempered with such animal hostility that the Kaneqians hadn't tried to make contact with them in recent history. The yetis' intellectual capabilities were greatly hampered by their love of killing and devouring almost anything that moved.

Bip, fighting his rising panic, thought of an escape plan. The yeti wasn't around at present, but Bip wouldn't make it four feet in the outside conditions if he were wet and naked. Thankfully, the yeti had stowed Bip's gear not too far from the pot. He reached over and began rummaging frantically through his pack, wondering what he could use to aid his escape. His sword? No point against a yeti. Bip had brief images of attacking a rock with a toothpick. Perhaps one of Glimton's reprogrammed acorns might be useful? But which one? He hadn't had time to see what they were all capable of...

Suddenly he heard the approaching thudding footsteps of his captor. He grabbed the first two items that came to hand and dived back into the pot. He looked down hopefully to see what he had retrieved. His face fell.

A thick corned beef sandwich and a bottle of Infamous Goose. *Great,* he thought, at *least I won't die hungry or sober...*

"Der you arr! Der you arr!" boomed the gravel-like voice of the yeti as it entered the room. "My littul munch treet. My littul man people stoo!" The yeti lowered its massive head until it looked right into Bip's eye. "Am gonner eet yerr!" it growled, then gave a conspiratorial wink.

Bip, too scared to react, merely sat there wide-eyed while the monster moved off and began pottering around what was evidentially its kitchen. It muttered to itself while it did so.

"Man peoples, man peoples. Don't eet much man peoples. Chewy, they sez, an' not much meat neevur. But the voicez, the voicez sez I gots to eet yer. So's am gonta eet yer."

Bip, his heart thudding somewhere up near his throat, could only nod in dumb agreement with whatever the mad beast was saying. He squirmed uncomfortably as he felt the temperature of the pot rise. The yeti continued its grumbling litany.

"But yer in luk. Yer in luk! Me Grundadz knew a recipe for man peoples—man peoples stoo, he called it. Sez it's da best fings he ever tasted. Man peoples stoo—proper pucka he said it was. Said it was *pucka*, he did."

Bip, who now couldn't help thinking about cookery as a distraction from his own inevitable cooking, began to think of a plan. A word had begun to formulate in his mind—a word and a subsequent escape plan. The word was *marinade...*

Slowly, so as not to draw attention to himself, Bip uncorked the bottle of Infamous Goose and sloshed it around in the pot water. The yeti didn't notice; it was busy talking to itself and crunching up vegetables with its tusks.

"Gots to pad em out with planties, me Grundad sed, coz there's not dat much meet. Gots to pad em out. Can't kill em neever. Gots to let em boil in der own blud. Can't have em leaking round the stew 'afore der time. Can't 'av dat. Its fer freshness is dat. Pucka! The voicez sez you is *pucka!*"

Bip began blinking rapidly, his eyes and nose streaming. They said that one sniff of Infamous Goose could get you merry. Bip, who was marinating in it, was already having trouble focusing. The yeti suddenly stopped its nonsensical monologue.

"Wot dats smell?" It began sniffing the air with its enormous bulbous nose, eventually reaching the cooking pot. It took a long whiff and made an appreciative gurgle.

"Youse is marinatin' nicely. *Nicely!*" said the yeti, then took a gigantic soup ladle down from the rack and tasted a generous measure of the cooking water. It stood briefly, its eyes slowly glazing over. "Pucka..." it burbled, before passing out on the floor with a terrific crash. Luckily for Bip, the yeti, though iron in its constitution when it came to eating, had never experienced the dubious delights of potent alcohol.

Thinking quickly, Bip leaped from the pot. It took him a while to get his balance, as floating in so much Infamous Goose had made him more than a little light-headed. He dried off as best he could with his traveling hat, donned his clothes, stacked his gear and was out of the yeti's cave in jig time.

He squinted as he came out into the bright white of the Ice Plains. By some incredible fortune, the yeti's lair was situated fairly close to the ice floes. Bip couldn't help but laugh. His abduction by the fearsome creature had, in a most unexpected way, turned out to be entirely beneficial. And all it had cost him was a bottle of Infamous Goose and a few mild heart attacks. Still, Bip didn't spend too long wondering about the oddities of fate, because no one wants to be around when a hungover yeti wakes up. He began jogging toward the floes, huffing a steady pace. This steady pace lasted for about five minutes until he heard the roar of an enraged and probably still drunk yeti coming from behind him. He began to sprint, his familiar litany of "Dammit, dammit, dammit, dammit!" a metronome for his pace.

The ice floes were very close. Bip risked a look behind him and was horrified to see that the yeti had covered a lot of ground, bounding on all fours with a look of fury on its shaggy face. Bip had no doubt he would reach the edge of the ice floes in time, but had a horrible suspicion he'd be killed and eaten before he could deploy the acorn boat.

He reached the edge of the ice floes and heard the thunderous approach of the monster behind him. With no other option, he turned around and drew Brian, ready to at least go out fighting. He gritted his teeth and tried not to wet himself as the yeti came closer...

Closer...

Suddenly there was a tremendous crack. The yeti skidded to a halt and looked around wildly, something resembling panic and confusion contorting its hairy face. Bip felt the ground under his feet lurch suddenly, and he waved his arms frantically to keep his balance. The yeti let out a howl of fear and disappeared into the ground.

It took Bip a while to realize what was going on. The ground he was standing on, near to the edge of the ice floes, had broken off from the mainland, dunking the scrabbling yeti into sub-zero waters. Bip fought the urge to laugh out loud as his own personal ice floe carried him away from the yeti's bubbling hollers. He tried to think of a choice one-liner to shout as he made his escape, but all he could think of was, "That's what you get for trying to eat me, you bastard!"

AS THE YETI slowly succumbed to the current of the icy water, it was, at the last, relieved when the maddening whispers in his head stopped.

Above it, on the shores of the ice floes, a figure popped into existence. It was annoyed. It had expected great things from the yeti. When you wanted a killing machine, you couldn't go far wrong with a yeti.

The figure thought to itself for a while, drumming its long fingers on its knees. "Oh well," it said. "There's more than one way to skin a cat." And with that, it popped out of existence. Then, instantaneously, a small bedraggled seagull took its place. The seagull chuckled to itself and took off after Bip's ice floe.

There's always more than one way to skin a cat. And none of them are pleasant.

Especially not for the cat.

10

Handen Strike and the Quest for the Fountain of Death

Handen Strike was annoyed. He was more than annoyed. He was *pissed off*.

It had been two years since he had left Kanick in the hopes of finding other civilizations. Two years since he had lost two of his closest friends to an angry Kraken. Two years since his feet had first touched the sands of the continent he currently resided on.

It had been a crappy two years.

His dilemmas had started when he had first scaled what had turned out to be known as the Molar Mountains. As well as an exhausting dangerous climb, Handen had encountered unfriendly dwarf tribes, cave-dwelling jeckles, and even an ill-tempered jabber-wocky that had attempted to feed him to its young. After leaving the mountains, he had crossed the Lightning Barrens, where, in his first encounter with what could pass as a civilized society, they had tried to burn him at the stake as a witch. After the Lightning Barrens, he had moved on to the Cotton Prairies, which, despite its friendly sounding name, had contained many, many things that had wanted to kill him, from packs of wickedly toothed dograbbits to the stomping, territorial uberbeast.

No. It had not been a good two years at all.

Not all of Handen's attempts at contacting civilization had been as entirely disastrous as his first. recognizing that telling people he was from another planet had not been a wise introductory tactic, Handen had simply decided to tell people he was a traveler and leave it at that. As the few settlements he had encountered on this new continent were spaced out and isolated, there had been no trouble in convincing the locals that he was merely from another village rather than another galaxy. He had survived comfortably over the long months by working where he could find it—mostly farmhand jobs, but enough to keep himself in food, shelter, and equipment. More often than not, he was moved along from the close-knit settlements by distrustful yeomanry, drifters being neither appreciated nor needed in villages that sometimes contained no more than a few families.

He never stayed in one place too long anyway, regardless of how comfortable the situation seemed. He still had his mission to think of and his priority was to find as large a concentration of people as possible before he risked telling anyone of Bersch's fate again. He needed access to the ears of people with influence and power—politicians or kings—and so far he had only encountered farmers and miners (unless you included the various goblins, hill giants, bloodthirsty monsters, zombies, and ghouls he had run into or away from, though he wasn't inclined to try to explain himself to them, and they had seemed even less inclined to listen).

He had tried, in ways both subtle and unsubtle, to learn as much as possible about the ruling powers of Bersch, though inevitably his questions brought hostile suspicion from the locals he stayed with, who led simple monotonous lives and distrusted elements of change. His prodding about cities and politics only brought dark mutterings about the mainland and no further elaborations. It had become evident that he was in a frontier country, not so much a civilization as a cluster of barely settled pilgrims doing the best they could to survive in inhospitable conditions. He would have to move on.

In his efforts to reach the mainland, Handen had eventually found his way south to Ghulbra Forest, into which, so he had heard, no one had ever ventured and been seen again. Not one to pay much attention to poorly founded native superstition, Handen had ventured into the massive forestland anyway. He had quickly begun to see the benefit of local wisdom when, after getting hopelessly lost, he had run into a tribe of heavily tattooed and uniformly bald forest-dwellers who were, apparently, extremely unreceptive to strangers.

They had been tracking him for five days.

Handen sighed. He didn't mind adventure. In fact, he loved adventure—it was his calling—but after two years of non-stop intrepid escapades, even the hardiest hero gets a little miffed.

Handen had changed a bit in the last two years. After countless fracas with hostile opponents and a lot of backbreaking farm labor, additional bulk had pumped up his already athletic frame. His features were swarthier, in need of a good shave, and his hair was a shaggy mockery of his former severe and uniform cut. He still wore his leather hunting overcoat, though it has been cut down to suit warmer temperatures, and the furs usually worn underneath had been replaced by the cotton shirt and trousers favored by the farm-folk. He had replaced his weapons, too, a coiled bullwhip at his side and a sturdy if primitive sword strapped across his backpack. They were nothing like as fine as the weapons he had lost to the sea so many months ago, but they look well-used and cared for. Handen Strike still cut quite an impressive figure, every inch the adventurer. The one thing spoiling his heroic demeanor at the moment was the fact that he was dangling helplessly by his bootstraps from a tree branch.

He hadn't meant to fall asleep in his hiding place, but five days on the run from the tireless pursuit of murderous savages had left him prone to napping whenever he lay still for more than a few seconds. Luckily, his boots had caught and saved him from a potentially fatal fall. Now all he had to do was get free before—

"(!) Nug mug, chug wub (!) clam!"

The primitive grunting Handen had come to dread sounded faintly through the forest. He stopped struggling and held his breath. They had found him! He had been convinced he was finally putting some real distance between them, yet here they were. Damn.

"(!) Pad gar. Gar pud. Pud!"

Handen gritted his teeth. In his less focused moments, he had begun to wonder if they were just making random noises and pretending it was language. It didn't seem like any actual form of communication at all, more a More Primal Than Thou conceitedness.

"(!) (!) (!) Pud!"

The voices were getting closer. Handen looked down from his precarious position to see three of the savages erupt soundlessly from the bushes and into the clearing directly below him. They walked carefully, as if they knew he was near, holding their longbows drawn and ready.

Handen continued to hold his breath, his heartbeat thudding in his ears. He was a sitting duck and he knew it. All he could do was pray that they didn't look up or that—

Crack!

A cynical part of Handen's soul had seen it coming a mile off. The branch supporting him first bent then snapped, sending him plummeting directly toward his pursuers. Fortunately, this meant that his fall was cushioned and gave the added bonus that he had half-crushed the people who had been trying to kill him. As they lay moaning on the floor, he seized his opportunity to run away.

Sprinting into the overgrown undergrowth he heard the telltale "(!)" of a very annoyed savage who had just been squashed and was now calling for his friends to avenge him. Behind him, far but not far enough, he heard the whooping of the hunters as they took up the chase.

Handen gritted his teeth, put his head down, and tried to increase his speed. This time he would outdistance them, find the time to cover his tracks and settle down in a hole in the ground until they got bored and went away. The savages had the advantage of knowing the territory, but Handen was a Hostility Advisor at the core and had been trained from birth for this sort of thing. He sprinted faster, pushing his way into thicker and thicker forest, jumping over moss-covered logs and ducking under thick, thorny branches. When the path ahead became too cluttered to travel through, Handen deftly flicked his bullwhip into the broad branches of the heavily entwined trees above him and swung himself onto higher ground. Once he found his balance, he began leaping and sprinting from tree to tree.

When Handen had first traveled into Ghulbra Forest, the surroundings had started as wood-like, then advanced to forest-like, until, at its unmapped core, it had resembled a mossy, decayed jungle. As a result, he found no trouble in running across the elevated pathways of interlocked branches, trunks, and canopies. He sprinted across the treetops until the voices behind him faded to nothing. Then he sprinted some more. He was, he had to admit, enjoying the chase. The heavy rain had finally cleared yesterday and now a pleasant sunshine was making the tree leaves glisten.

If I'm going to be hunted down and killed by bloodthirsty savages who want to eat my brain, thought Handen, *then at least it'll be a nice day for it.*

He leaped from a treetop and managed to hook his bullwhip around a neighboring branch, then, swinging with animal grace, he used his momentum to launch himself up onto an even higher branch. Breathing heavily, he surveyed the woods to his rear and smiled with smug satisfaction. There was no sign of his pursuers yet, and if he hid himself, they would have serious difficulty finding him. All he would have to do was—

Crack!

Handen had time to curse silently as he fell through the air, the branch that had formerly supported him spinning out of his eye-line.

Yep. It had been a crappy two years.

BIP WAS BORED. He was also thirsty, hungry, sunburnt, and badly in need of a bath. But he was, primarily, bored.

He had begun his sea voyage in a very good mood, with the adrenaline high of escaping the yeti still fresh in his veins. He had dunked the "BOAT" acorn into the seawater and watched with amazement as the reprogrammed seed had planted itself and begun to grow quickly into a small vessel, looking like a giant, hollowed out acorn shell with a sail of woven bracken. Madman or not, there was no doubting the quality of Glimton's handiwork.

The boat had sailed a good pace on the iron-gray ocean and had so far steered clear of any bad weather, holding a slow but steady southward course.

However, the voyage had begun over four weeks ago, and now Bip was not so pleased with his progress. He was running worryingly low on food and water and, not knowing how long he would remain at sea, had long since taken to rationing himself.

Worse still, the weather had turned oppressively hot, meaning that during the day it was too stuffy to stay in the small shelter he had made from his oilskin. As a result of this, Bip was currently sitting cross-legged on the foredeck, naked, badly sunburned, and with his sea-soaked underpants wrapped around his head to combat the heavy beat of the sun. He was beginning to wonder if he was getting sunstroke but could not yet face the prospect of lying in the muggy shelter. At least here, on what could loosely be called the prow of the acorn vessel, there was a slightly cooling breeze.

His biggest problem, though, was the boredom. He had been on his own so long he was even nostalgic for the yeti's company, and quite recently he had taken to talking to himself. He wasn't sure if he was happy with that development and frequently said so. To himself.

In darker moments, he had thought of settling down with the last bottle of Infamous Goose and spending a few days getting roaring drunk. It would dehydrate him further, he knew, and possibly make him very ill, but it would relieve some of the oppressive boredom. He was sick of the sea. Sick of how blue it was. Sick of how endless it was. He would shout sarcastically at the waves, chiding their monotonous up and down movements, cursing their lack of imagination. He would plead with the horizon, begging it to throw up some sort of distraction. He had tried fishing, sticking a small lump of corned beef sandwich on the end of a ripped sock, but so far, no fish had found the prospect of a corned beef flavored sock exciting enough to take a bite.

He was sick of the sound of the wind, which seemed to flap the organic sail in an unpredictable and unexpected pattern of noise, its stubborn refusal to yield to any kind of rhythm nearly equivalent to someone singing deliberately off-key. He was sick of the sky, which unlike the bulbous, gray clouds that mingled endlessly above the Ice Plains, was a stark and featureless steel of blue, altering only to make way for a painful, retina-burning glare that Bip could only assume was where the sun resided. He was sick of boats and quests and everything. He wanted to go home.

"I'll die out here," he said to himself, glumly. "I'll never reach land and I'll just die. Here in the middle of nowhere. I wonder if this is how all the other volunteers died?"

"Cheer up, mug!" came a voice from nowhere.

Bip was surprised. It hadn't been his voice, and he was the only person he'd talked to in weeks.

"What did I say?" he muttered dreamily.

"Not you, chump, me! Up here!"

Bip looked at the front of the boat. Sitting there like some mad-eyed figurehead was a dirty looking seagull.

"Did you just say something?" said Bip.

"Cower and despair as the very core of madness engulfs you," said the seagull, matter-of-factly.

Bip seemed to contemplate doing so for a minute, and then went back to staring glumly at the horizon. The seagull seemed fairly annoyed by this and hopped about until it was in front of Bip's face.

"Well?" it shrieked irritably. "Aren't you going to freak out? Aren't you going to start banging your head and tearing at your hair and screaming that you've lost your mind?"

Bip looked up, puzzled. "No," he said. "Why? Should I?"

"Yes, because you're talking to a seagull, you cretin, and when you're not talking to a seagull, you're talking to yourself!"

"Exactly," Bip said. "Talking to you is much more interesting. If I start complaining about being insane, you might go away—then I'll have no one to talk to but me."

The seagull flapped its wings in irritation. "No! No, no, no! You're not really talking to me. I'm just a symptom of your growing dementia and continuing despair! Doesn't that bother you?"

"Not really," muttered Bip. "It's more interesting than being sane and bored. Besides, I expect I'm not insane at all. I expect this is just a bizarre fever-dream bought on by too much sun."

"No, really, trust me. You're demented. You're mad. You're a couple of cattle short of a herd!"

"Why should I believe you? You're just a seagull!"

The seagull hopped up and down in feathery rage. "But that's just the point! I'm not a bloody seagull, am I? I'm a bloody metaphor, you thick-headed idiot!"

"A metaphor for what?" said Bip.

The seagull gave a long and croaky sigh. "Well, you see, seagulls only come out to sea to die? So I'm, like, an omen. A symbol of your impending and lonely death, urging you to turn back and go home."

"I can't turn around," said Bip. "I can't steer the boat. Besides, I thought running into seagulls meant you were near land?"

"Well. Yes," conceded the gull. "But in this case, I'm a symbol of lonely, horrible death!"

"I don't know," said Bip doubtfully. He squinted at the horizon. "That sort of looks like land to me."

The seagull looked in the direction Bip indicated, flapping its wings to get a better view.

"Bugger," it said, and vanished with a pop.

"Well I'll be jiggered," muttered Bip. "Land." Then he fell over and lost consciousness.

IT MAY or may not be worth mentioning that at this point, many fathoms below Bip, the Kraken awoke from its slumber. It was very old these days and, having long since established itself as the most dangerous predator in this stretch of the ocean, had settled down to have a family.

It sensed the presence of the intruding boat above it, a feeling it had not felt for nearly a thousand years, and thought briefly about attacking. Then it looked down at the four suckling Krakoids at its teat and thought better of it.

It scratched at the scars on its throat and chest, remembering the encounter with the last boat that had been near its territory. It was getting too old to take risks these days, and it was tough enough as it was being a single mum without inviting additional injuries. The Kraken briefly wished it hadn't been forced to eat the father nearly five hundred years ago. Oh well. It was a cold, cold ocean and you had to do the best you could.

HANDEN AWOKE. His head hurt.

The last few minutes he remembered were something of a blur. He had fallen from the tree and the ground had rushed up to meet him, but before he had hit, his belt strap had caught on a vine, swinging him into some dark and muddy glade. He had slid down a slope for what had seemed to be ages, then eventually, muddy, dizzy, and exhausted, he had come to a halt and fallen into a deep sleep.

He looked around. He was in a sunny clearing. The trees towered thickly around him. Here and there throughout the tall grass, lumps of stone that could have been statues leaned casually against one another. Handen was still fuzzy-headed from his ordeal. He had no idea how long he had been sleeping and no idea where he was. That was why, when he saw the small, sparkly lake that bubbled out of an underground spring, he didn't think twice about drinking deeply, quenching a thirst that had been building steadily over five days of hot pursuit. The water was refreshing and ice-cold, with a mineral tang that set his teeth on edge.

It wasn't until he had finished drinking long and hard that he had the presence of mind to take a closer look at his surroundings. That was when he noticed the ominous slab of stone with the indecipherable hieroglyphics that stood near the center of the lake. "Oh, damn," he muttered.

Handen had no idea what the carvings said but was beginning to realize he was on what appeared to be holy ground—and holy ground nearly always meant trouble. He froze instantly, attuning his senses to the world around him. He stood stock still, remaining absolutely rigid for nearly five minutes in a state of high-strung alertness. Then relaxed. So far, no spears, no rolling balls of stone, no one calling him "infidel." In Handen's book, these were all good signs.

He took another moment to explore his new surroundings. The clearing was peaceful and quiet. He felt as relaxed here as he had done for nearly two years. He lay back on the grass and listened to the far-off birdsong.

That was when he heard the snoring.

He bolted upright and flipped onto his feet, sword in hand before he had even realized it. The steady rhythmical snoring was coming from somewhere close. Silently, he stalked around the clearing in an attempt to locate the source of the noise. Eventually, he came to a squat stone building, heavily encased in vines, sporting only a small door and window. He relaxed slightly and sneaked up to the window to get a closer look. There, lying on a stone slab and looking quite elegant (apart from the farmyard-like snoring,) was an attractive woman in a white robe, her golden hair held back by a ring of silver. Handen, who had not seen a woman in weeks, was impressed by the sleeper's beauty. He thought for a while, then reached a decision. He would risk contact with the woman.

After all, he thought, *I'm sure I'm due to meet someone who doesn't want to kill me eventually.*

He walked up to the door and noticed a length of rope with some more hieroglyphics carved into the stone behind it. Shrugging, Handen pulled the rope.

There was a *bing.* Followed by a *bong.* The snoring stopped abruptly.

Handen tensed as the door opened. Before him stood the woman he had seen on the slab. She stretched and rubbed her eyes and completely failed to try to kill him. "Good morning," she said in an attractively chirpy voice. "How may I help you?"

Handen floundered. In truth, he had been expecting her to shout something about infidels and try to set fire to him. Offering services was completely out of the blue.

"Let me guess." The woman smiled. "You're an adventurer, yes?"

Handen nodded—he couldn't deny it. He seemed to have been plagued by countless adventures lately.

"And you drank from the fountain, yes?"

Handen nodded again.

The woman's demeanor changed suddenly. Her eyes glazed, and her smile widened. She began to speak as though reading from some internal script.

"Allow me to be the first to congratulate you on your newfound immortality, and I hope, as a patron of the fountain of youth, you will adhere to the vows of supreme secrecy and will consider joining our gold card members club for the low, low price of five tillers a month. My name is Tanya, and I'm here to answer any questions you may have. Have a nice day!" said Tanya. Then, so suddenly that even Handen's quick reactions couldn't stop her, she drew a wicked-looking knife from her robe and plunged it into the adventurer's heart.

Handen screamed in pain and horror as she pulled the knife back. He fell to the floor as blood flowed at a frightening pace from his chest wound. As the searing agony faded into a numb nothing, Handen sat back and waited to die, staring dumbly at his chest.

He waited.

Eventually he wondered what the hell was going on. He felt his chest, bracing for a pain that didn't come. Underneath the sticky gore on his shirt, the chest wound had disappeared.

"Sorry about that," said Tanya. "Most people don't believe me about the 'immortal' part. That's just a quick way of convincing people. I could do it again if you like?"

Handen shook his head rapidly and got to his feet. "What the hell is going on?" he shouted.

Tanya sighed and rolled her eyes. "It's quite simple. Didn't you read the ancient hieroglyphics? You've found the fountain of youth! After years of fruitless searching, no doubt."

"I wasn't looking for any damn fountain," growled Handen. "I was just trying to find my way out of this stinking forest!"

Tanya gasped. "You mean you didn't know? Oh dear. This hasn't happened before. Normally when people find this place they're ecstatic. They don't usually start getting annoyed about it for another couple of centuries."

"What? What other people?" said Handen, struggling to keep up with things.

"You didn't think you were the first person to find the fountain of youth, did you?" giggled Tanya. "Oh, no. Lots of people have found it! I was one of them!"

"So you're immortal, are you?" said Handen.

"Oh, yes," said Tanya. "I must be nearly eight hundred years old by now."

Quick as a flash, Handen drew his sword and beheaded the woman in one blurring swipe. The head rose into the air in a jet of arterial spray and landed on the ground, where it rolled to a stop and began spitting dust out of its mouth. The body put it hands on its hips.

"Well!" said Tanya's head. "You didn't have to do that!"

"Just checking," Handen muttered.

Tanya's body picked up Tanya's head and placed it back on its neck. The wound began to heal almost instantly, sticky tendrils of flesh interweaving with each other until it was impossible to tell that she had recently been decapitated.

"See?" she said. "Immortal! Although that was still very rude!"

"Sorry," burbled Handen, swaying on his feet. "I'm a bit new to this."

Tanya nodded in sympathy. "Tell you what, why don't you come inside and have a nice cup of tea?"

<hr>

"OF COURSE, the good thing about being immortal is that you spend a lot less money on skin care products," said Tanya as she poured Handen another cup.

Handen nodded dumbly.

The inside of the stone hut was decorated quite nicely, in a tasteless sort of way. The rock walls were adorned with flowery curtains, and the single stone table was awash with doilies. It was clear that whoever had decorated had struggled to imprint a sense of homeliness on what was, essentially, a cave.

"It gets boring, mind you," continued Tanya. "That's why I took this job. You just sleep for a few hundred years, waiting for the next immortal. You show them the ropes, as it were, until someone comes to relieve you. It's very peaceful, but I'm pretty sure someone's due to relieve me soon."

Handen nodded dumbly.

"I expect someone will be along any time now. That's what you do when you get tired of living—you either come here or you search for the fountain of death."

Handen nodded dumbly.

Then he frowned. "Wait a minute. Fountain of death?"

"Mmm-hmm, that's right. It's the only thing that can kill an immortal, or so they say. Of course, no one's ever found it, or if they have, they haven't lived to talk about it. Obviously." Tanya sipped her tea.

Handen continued to stare into space. He was entertaining a terrible inner vision, an image of being immortal, un-killable, when the planet of Bersch exploded. Drifting through space for a possible eternity…

"Right then," he said. "I'm off."

"Where are you going?" said Tanya.

"I'm going to save the planet, then I'm going to find the fountain of death."

"Wait, wait, wait!" squealed Tanya. Then she reached into her pocket and brought out a gold brooch, which she placed on Handen's chest. There was a brief flash and a burning sensation. Handen looked inside his shirt to see a small tattoo of a snake eating its own tail, twisting at its middle to form a figure-of-eight shape.

"What's this?" he demanded.

"That's the mark of the immortal," said Tanya. "We've all got one." She pulled up the hem of her robe to reveal a nearly identical mark to Handen's on her calf. "Quite fetching, I think." She giggled.

"Yes. I suppose," said Handen, gruffly.

"Oh, and you might need these." She shoved an armload of rolled-up parchment into Handen's backpack.

"What are they?" he said.

"Maps," replied Tanya. "They're a good few centuries out of date, but they might be helpful."

Handen nodded his thanks and made to leave.

"One more thing!" said Tanya suddenly.

Handen's burning impatience was doused a little as he turned to look at his fellow immortal. She was beautiful and would remain beautiful for the rest of her existence, but there was a dullness in her eyes, a pained tiredness that belonged in the skull of a dying old woman. Handen felt a sudden shiver in his spine.

"If you find the fountain of death," said Tanya, "you will come back and tell me where it is, won't you?"

11

Bolan Cay

It was barely an island, and if it was an island, it would be the kind of island that all the other islands picked on. It was a golden stretch of sand that was nearly thirty meters across in either direction, dotted in the surrounding sea like a speck of dust on a blue-tinted mirror. It didn't boast much scenery bar the occasional jutting rock on its meager coastline and a lonely cluster of palm trees at its center, but it did have a populace of seagulls, who hung around in seedy gangs, sneering and cawing aggressively at one another.

The most spectacular feature of the almost-island was the tiny wooden hut that sat in the limited shade. That is not to say that the hut was spectacular in any way other than being more interesting than the trees and seagulls that surrounded it. From the hut emerged the hunched frame of a man, dressed in a flowery shirt and sunglasses and a wide-brimmed straw hat. He yawned and stretched, his ancient, chubby features long ago sunburned to a merry pink. Smacking his lips under the short straggles of his sun-bleached beard, he surveyed his domain.

And paused. Frowning. Not sure if what he was seeing was really there.

Floundering briefly in the sand, he rushed back into his hut and returned moments later with two wooden poles, a banner, and a table. Hurriedly, he propped the poles and table in the sand and attached the banner, which read, "Bolan Cay Tourist Information Center." The man stood underneath the banner, smiling a wide and welcoming smile. He smiled for a few minutes. Eventually he got bored and wandered over to the focus of his attention.

A small, organic-looking ship was bobbing relentlessly against the sands of Bolan Cay. Its bark-like hull was stuck fast, its bush-like sail flapping uselessly in the slight breeze. The man approached cautiously, wondering why the ship appeared deserted. He looked over the prow of the vessel to see a disheveled-looking young man sprawled across the ship's deck. The young man didn't look at all well. His glasses were skew-whiff on his small blunt nose, and his closely cropped hair was windswept and ruffled. His skin had burned a pink to rival the older man's own.

The man seemed a little disappointed, but nevertheless he hoisted the sparse frame of the shipwrecked stranger and, with a lot of effort, dragged him back to the hut.

BIP'S EYELIDS, after a trying struggle with the gloop that had been holding them closed, managed to pry themselves apart. The light was cool, and a pleasant salty smell hung in the stock-still air. Bip could feel a mattress of some sort beneath him and comfortable fabric covering his body. His ears detected the lulling sound of arguing seagulls. All in all, Bip's senses were reporting very good things. All except his sense of taste, which was telling him that his mouth was as dry, foul, and unpleasant as the world's oldest gym sock.

He croaked.

"You're awake, then?" said a voice. "I guess you'd like a glass of water, yeah?"

Bip croaked in the affirmative, too thirsty to be concerned about to whom the voice belonged. He was given a glass of fresh but lukewarm water, which he gulped greedily. A few more glasses were passed and drunk before Bip had the presence of mind to see just who his generous host actually was. He looked at the old man and tried to form a sentence. His head was still buzzy from too much sun.

"What would you like first?" said the old man. "The 'who are you?' or the 'where am I?'"

Bip considered briefly. "'S'pose the 'where am I?' is more conventional."

"Bing! Two points!" said the old man, with just a little more enthusiasm than Bip was ready for. "Two points, yessiree, 'where am I?' indeed! Well, I'll tell you where you are! You're in the Free Country's greatest, latest, and most secluded holiday resort—Bolan Cay!"

Bip scratched his head and squinted at the old man. He kept on getting distracted by the loudness of his shirt and the whiteness of his teeth. "Am a what now?" he managed.

"Yep, Bolan Cay. Heaven on Bersch! Do you sometimes need to get away from it all?" said the old man, leaning over and putting a conspiratorial and sympathetic arm around Bip's shoulders. Bip considered the question, but wasn't given the opportunity to reply.

"Sure ya do, sure ya do! The hustle and bustle of city life? Early morning traffic? Problems with the horse and cart? Boss don't give you time off for plague? Yeah, we all know that story, but don't let the yeoman get you down—come to Bolan Cay! Where seclusion and tranquility are a way of life! (Monsoon season excluded, tranquility not guaranteed.)"

Bip blinked a few times while various words and exclamation marks kicked him in the ear hole. "I'm sorry. What?" he said.

The old man continued, unfazed by Bip's apparent lack of enthusiasm. "We've got the finest food this side of the Empire. Don't forget to try our seagull on rye, soup de la seagull, and seagull surprise! Mmm-mmm—surprisingly seagully! And why not wash it down with a fresh, cool water cocktail? Then relax and enjoy one of the island's many cabaret acts!" The old man whipped out what looked like a pygmy guitar and plucked a few notes. It sounded exactly as you would expect a pygmy guitar to sound.

Bip rubbed his eyes. "I'm sorry, but I have no clue what you're on about," he said.

The old man's huge grin faded to a merely large grin. "Am I to assume you are not, shall we say, in the market for leisure and tourism?"

Bip thought about it. "No. I suppose not."

"Then get the hell out of my bed!" growled the old man. "And gimme that!" he added, taking the half full glass of water from Bip's hands.

Bip was quickly ushered back outside and into the glaring sunshine, the old man prodding and pushing him all the way.

"You got some nerve taking up space in a five-star resort such as this and not even being a tourist!" he shouted, his face even pinker than usual.

"I'm very sorry, I'm sure," said Bip, taking in his surroundings, "but I thought this was just a wooden hut in the middle of a bit of sand."

The old man looked at first confused, then angry, then he flopped down in the sand with a sigh of resignation. "You're right, of course," he said. "But we all gotta have a dream, don't we?"

Bip, who during his training had developed something of a soft spot for unpredictable mood swings, sat down next to the old man and patted him reassuringly on the shoulder. "There, there," he said, in the worried tones of someone who has never believed people actually said "there, there" but is now saying it nonetheless.

"I'm Bolan, by the way," said the old man. "This is my island." He gestured half-heartedly around the weedy stretch of sand. On the shore, two seagulls fought noisily over a rock that looked a bit like a fish.

"It's very…nice," ventured Bip. "Very…peaceful?"

"Really?" said Bolan, brightening up. "You think so? Because that's what I keep telling people. I even put it on the brochure: 'Peace, tranquility, seclusion—Bolan Cay's got tons of each!' Nothing but ocean for miles around! No distractions at all!"

"You're right there," said Bip, as anything interesting completely failed to happen.

"I woulda thought that with all the problems with the Empire back on the mainland, people would be queuing up for a bit of peace and tranquility!" said Bolan.

"Problems? Empire?" prompted Bip, who recognized a bit of quest-advancing information when he saw it.

"Why sure! You don't know about the Empire? Used to be that those who didn't like the way the Argustin Empire did things could scoot on over to the Free Countries, you know? But these days, the Free Countries ain't so free, if you get my meaning?"

"Yeah," said Bip, who didn't, but disliked interrupting people when they were in full verbal flow.

"Yep," said Bolan. "I figured I'd open my island to the public, give people a chance to escape tyranny and oppression for a couple of weeks for the knock-down price of... Ah, whadda you care?" he finished. "You're no tourist." Bolan looked glumly at the sand, unaware of just how much of an understatement "tourist" was when applied to Bip.

Bip looked thoughtful for a moment. "I think I need to get to the Empire," he said.

Bolan raised his bushy eyebrows. "You *want* to go to the Empire?" He shook his hoary head in disbelief. "Kids," he muttered.

"I think that's where I need to go. Can you tell me how to get there?" said Bip.

Bolan laughed. "You can't miss it, kid; the Empire covers three quarters of the globe! But if you mean the heart of the Empire, Argustin, then you have to get to the mainland, Regalious—and to do that you have to sail farther south to the Free Countries. It's not far—a coupla days should get you to Port Town." The old man stopped himself. "But you don't wanna go to Port Town, kid. Nothing there but robbers, thieves, and other types that steal stuff."

"Will someone there be able to tell me how to get to the capital?"

"Oh, undoubtedly," said Bolan, gruffly. "If you've got enough gold on you."

Bip, who did in fact have a huge lump of gold in his rucksack, got to his feet.

"Mr. Bolan," he said, "I appreciate your hospitality and regret I cannot stay on your lovely island, but I really have to get to the Empire. Would you give me a hand casting off my boat?"

Bolan sighed. "Kids," he muttered. "Always in a hurry. Anyone would think the world was coming to an end…"

WITH A BIT of effort and a few grazed shins, Bolan and Bip managed to maneuver the acorn boat to the south side of the island and cast off. Bolan watched as Bip bobbed out into the sea, enough fresh water on the boat to last him comfortably to the Free Countries.

"Hey, kid," Bolan shouted. "I forgot to ask; where did you come from anyway?"

"The North," Bip called back. "From the Ice Plains!"

"That's crazy! Nobody comes from the Ice Plains. Everyone knows it's nothing but a big patch of snow and ice. Full o' dangerous animals too. Ain't no one steps foot on the Ice Plains by choice!"

"Yeah, that's pretty much true!" Bip shouted. "Goodbye!"

"And don't forget!" yelled Bolan. "Tell your friends about Bolan Cay! More peace and quiet than a sane man can handle!"

Bip waved back. Bolan watched as the acorn boat faded into a dot, then he watched the horizon for a few hours. There was really nothing better to do.

FAR OUT INTO SPACE, the Massive Ball of Death raced on. The civilization that had spawned it had long since expired, their short-lived cease-fire ending in a catastrophic war that had eventually killed them all, but the Massive Ball of Death lived on as a legacy.

It was vaguely aware of this somehow. After traveling countless miles for countless years, being bombarded with all kinds of cosmic rays and radiation from across the universe, the nuclear cluster was developing sentience of a sort. It was aware that it was going in what it had chosen to perceive as a "forward" direction and that eventually "forward" had to run out. Knowing this made it feel a faint imitation of optimism. Thus, the universe's most chirpy ball of ice, dust, radiation, and nuclear armaments continued to roll across the inky void of space, causing paranoia and chaos wherever it did go.

A particular group of people blissfully unaware that they were in the path of said Massive Ball of Death were currently celebrating another successful bout of swashbuckling thievery and adventure by the tried and tested method of drinking beyond reasonable capacity. The *S.S. Blunderbuss* swayed merrily in the orbit of a small moon, its gun turrets firing periodically to the beat of a jaunty tune. Inside, Captain Kwiksave Lombardo, pirate king and the galaxy's most intrepid freebooter, stood on a table, trying to hold three bottles of gut rot in one hand and using his other to conduct a merry (if unspeakably dirty) pirate tune with a cigar.

Some called him No Beard, others The Prince of Scum. Some people called him the Space Cowboy, others called him a Galactic Pain in the Bum. By any name, Kwiksave Lombardo was the most infamous of all space pirates, and his latest raid had been a fantastic success. The booty had been bountiful, and his merry men were very merry indeed.

The tune came to a predictable conclusion, and the men toasted their victory for the seventy-ninth time so far before falling about in general good-humored slobbishness.

One man managed to pick himself up from the floor. "Sing us a song, Cap'n!" he cried.

"Aye!" agreed another, paused to belch massively, then said, "Let's hear a song from the pirate king!" A raucous cheer went up, although to be fair, the crew would've cheered anything in their current state.

"Now, now, boys," said Kwiksave. "Now. Now. Now? What? No… erm…" He swayed for a while, trying to figure out what he had been going to say. A light of recollection shone suddenly in his one eye. "Yes! A song! I mean, no! I don't want to. I'm self-conscious…"

"Self-conscious?" bellowed the first mate, a cyborg by the proud old robot name of KillCrushDestroy. "Self-conscious? The man who once took on the evil, eight-armed Octomen of Premidin Prime in a duel to the death, blindfolded, and came out unscathed?"

The crew cheered while Captain Lombardo flapped his arms with drunken modesty.

"The man who once seduced the goddess-like Queen of Shebara, the holiest of virgins with a face that launched a billion ships, then refused to give her his phone number afterward!?"

The crew cheered. Captain Lombardo continued to flap.

"The man who once stole the wallet of the Zebirom Death Lord and used his credit cards to order embarrassing products that he then had delivered to the Death Lord's mum's house? Self-conscious?"

The crew cheered.

"Now, now, Mr. KillCrushDestroy! You're embarrassing me!" said Kwiksave.

"Oh, go on, Captain! Sing that song you sing about being the pirate king!"

The crew whooped appreciatively.

"Oh, okay, then," said Kwiksave. "If I must."

The crew hollered joyfully for a while, then hushed themselves to an attentive silence. Kwiksave prepared to sing his song.

"*Weeellll…*" he began.

But then the SS blunderbuss was struck by the wake of the Massive Ball of Death and was sent crashing down to the moon's surface.

Kwiksave was first up after the rumbling noises had stopped. He looked about the smoky cabin, lit by the sparking of important-looking equipment. He began to bark orders.

"Recalibrate the oxytron matrix fiddler!"

"Aye, Cap'n!"

"Configure the atmospheric stabilizer!"

"Aye, Cap'n!"

"Reboot the warp flux confligulater!"

"We don't have one, Cap'n!"

"Then remind me to bloody well get one!"

"Aye, Cap'n!"

"What the hell was that?" said Captain Lombardo, after the chaos had been brought to an acceptable level of control.

"I may be wrong about this, Cap'n," said KillCrushDestroy, "but it looked to me like a huge cluster of nuclear weapons covered in space dust."

Lombardo thought for a while. "Then all things considered, that could have been a lot worse," he concluded.

He turned back to the crew, each of them scared sober and looking for leadership. "Now," he said. "Where the hell is my cigar?"

Far out into space, the Massive Ball of Death kept on going, aware, in a good-humored kind of way, that nothing was going to stop it.

12

Port Town

The beach was a mournful place, moping gloomily across the shore like an old picture etched in charcoal. Bone-white sand stretched from horizon to horizon, interrupted here and there by the black of rotting seaweed, age-old driftwood, and murky-looking rock pools. Jagged gray stones reached up toward a jagged gray sky, defiant totems of sharpness on the smudged and lackluster scenery. In the distance, a white cliff toed the line between ground and sky, while the foggy ghosts of enormous flat-headed mountains squashed the horizon. A faint wind blew with a deceptive volume, mixing with the white noise of the breaking waves to create a sound like old memories.

This was not a beach where people would come to relax. This was more like a beach where poets might come to kill themselves.

Such a brooding topography, it seemed, had no place for people. Yet a person was there, dressed in a texture of purple and black that complemented and even competed with the neighboring gloom. As silent as a painting, the figure stood in a solitude well worthy of his surroundings.

Azron Bezron hung out by the shore. In fact, he didn't so much hang as drape. Slouched against a rock on the driftwood-cluttered beach, he struggled to light a cigarette against the chill breeze from the sea.

There are various words to describe Azron, none of them particularly nice. "Suspicious" is perhaps the least offensive. His stick-thin frame pointed at its joints, adding razor angles to the long, shapeless coat that brushed against the ground. A pointy face with pointy sideburns, a pointy moustache, and a small pointy goatee pointed out from under a peak-less woolen hat. A permanent pointy grin revealed the slightly crooked teeth of a very crooked man. Dark, oily features surrounded a pair of eyes that shifted about in the confident, good-humored way of a man who knows the world is there to be taken…for the right pair of hands.

Azron Bezron was a thief. A damn good one. Like his father and his father's father. And his mother. And his aunt, sister, little brother Maslo, cousin Deek, Uncle "Fingers"… In fact, pretty much everyone Azron had ever known had been a thief.

Currently he was stealing a bit of time for himself, relaxing on the shore a comfortable distance from the constant challenge of Port Town. He gazed out to sea and lost himself in a daydream.

A small speck appeared on the horizon. Azron's lazy half-smile crawled further up the side of his face. He waited with an easy patience until the speck turned into a boat. Then he waited some more. Eventually the boat reached the shore, and Azron watched as a scrawny figure attempted to moor it to the skeleton of a long-ago beached vessel. Azron grinned at the futility of the activity. Tie or no tie, the boat would not be there tomorrow. Someone would have nicked it.

The scrawny figure began to approach, revealing a lad in his late teens. Azron took in his unusual clothing: the wide-brimmed traveling hat, the delicate half-moon glasses, the over-stuffed backpack, and the sword scabbard at his side. Somewhere in Azron's brain, a calculation took place.

"All right, mate?" said Azron, still puffing at his thin cigarette.

"Yes," said Bip. "I wonder if you could tell me where I am?"

Azron considered the question for a while before seemingly disregarding it completely. Instead of answering, he re-lit his faltering cigarette and said, "We don't get many people sailing in from the Cold Ocean. In fact, I think you're about the first one I've ever seen. Where did you say you were from, sunshine?"

"I didn't," said Bip, who was feeling mildly disconcerted. Azron had an unusual way of talking to people. He would maintain eye contact very briefly before shifting his gaze about the place, as though expecting someone to sneak up on him. Half the time it appeared that Azron was addressing someone behind him rather than the person he was actually talking to. Coupled with his odd habit of speaking quietly through the side of his mouth, a conversation with Azron often left people with a sense of general paranoia.

"I'll rephrase it, shall I?" said Azron. "Where've you come from?"

"Oh. I sailed here from the Ice Plains."

Azron fixed Bip with a beady stare. "Yeah," he muttered. "And I'm the bloody Emperor."

"Really?" said Bip, excitedly. "What an enormous stroke of luck, because, you see, you're the very man I've been looking for!"

Azron looked blank for a while. "I'm not the Emperor."

"But you just said—"

"Look, mate, nobody comes from the Ice Plains. Nobody goes to the Ice Plains. You'd have to cross miles and miles of monster-infested waters, where, or so it's said, behemoths from the dawn of creation still roam freely."

Bip stood in contemplation for a moment. "Can't say I saw any behemoths, exactly."

"Through chaotic winds that cause waves the size of castles to crash down on the unsuspecting sailor."

"Well, it got a bit choppy coming in to the shore…"

"Where storms rage with such terrible madness that the very sound of the thunder will turn a man's mind to mush."

"No. No, sorry. I didn't see anything like that, really."

Azron looked disappointed. "So what terrible perils did you face then, guv?"

Bip thought for a moment. "There was a seagull," he concluded.

"A seagull."

"Yes. And I got a bit sunburnt."

Azron peered suspiciously at Bip. "Well, mate, you're either the worst liar I've ever met or you're telling the truth. Either way, this is Melan Cove."

Bip looked around. As bleak as Melan Cove seemed, it was a carnival of color compared to the shore he had originally left.

"Can you tell me if I'm anywhere near Port Town?" said Bip.

Azron grinned his lazy grin. "And what does a chap like you want in a place like Port Town?" he said, jetting cigarette smoke through his nostrils.

"Information, mainly," said Bip. "I need to know how to get to the heart of the Empire."

Azron looked at Bip for a long while. "I'll give you some advice for free, mate; we don't talk loose about the Empire, right? 'Specially not in Port Town."

"...Yes?" said Bip.

"You're really not from around here, are you?" said Azron, an appraising look in his eye.

"No! I told you, I'm from the Ice Plains."

"Yeah, yeah. The Ice Plains, right." Azron stared thoughtfully into space and began rubbing his chin as his crooked grin etched slowly across his dark features. Bip began to feel quite uncomfortable.

"I tell you what, mate, this is your lucky day!" he said finally.

"Really?" replied Bip.

"Yes, because for a nominal fee, as a one-time only offer, I can be your guide to and around Port Town for the duration of your visit, like." Azron smiled smugly.

Bip thought for a moment. "That would be brilliant," he concluded.

"Yeah, yeah, brilliant," said Azron, his grin stretching further across his thin face. "You know, I think this could be the start of something great!"

THE TWO TRAVELERS sat in the back of the rickety merchant wagon they had managed to hitch a ride with as they made their way to Port Town. The scenery around the wagon trail was a marked improvement on Melan Cove, the depressing sand drifts of which had eventually given way to wide passes of green with faint bumps of hillsides here and there.

They were currently following a wide river, where large, bumping barges floated ceaselessly back and forth, laden with cargo of all descriptions.

"Obviously we get no trade from the Cold Ocean," said Azron, who was chattering idly about the commerce of Port Town, "but more often than not, it's far easier to sail goods around the coasts and through the rivers than it is to cart them about."

Bip nodded. He was greatly impressed by the various boats and barges. This wasn't difficult, of course, as the only boat Bip had any real experience of had grown from an acorn.

"That's why Port Town is called Port Town, see?" continued Azron, raising his voice slightly over the rattle of the wagon's axels. "It's situated where all the rivers converge closest to the sea. A trade hub, sort of thing."

"So is that what you do, then, Azron?" said Bip. "Trade things?"

"Yeah, sort of," replied Azron. "Sort of like trading, except when people 'give' me things, I generally don't give them anything back, like."

"Isn't that just stealing?" said Bip, frowning.

"Well, yes," said Azron. "That's what we do in Port Town. We steal things. Everybody steals things. It's the way things are done."

"So you're a thief, then?" said Bip.

"Not just any thief, mate, I'm one of the big shots. I'm a Diamond Geezer, me. First class and all," said Azron, his narrow chest swelling with pride.

"I'm sorry, what?" said Bip.

Azron produced a wallet and took out a card. It was an elaborate certificate embossed with the legend "Port Town Union of Dodgy

Fellows". Beneath it was Azron's mugshot, bearing the caption, "Genuine Diamond Geezer (1st class)."

"Diamond Geezer? You know? They don't come much better than me, sunshine, let me tell you. Most people in Port Town are lucky if they can make it to a third-class mugger, or a bronze-level rogue, but me? Diamond-level Geezer, mate! Not bronze, not silver, and not gold, but diamond. Means I'm recognized by the union as a top-level geezer, if you know what I mean?"

"No," said Bip.

"I'm a geezer. Jack-of-all-trades, sort of thing. Grifting, pick-pocketing, shoplifting, breaking, and entering. I've done them all, mate. When it comes to down-and-outs, I'm right up there at the top!"

Bip was shocked. "So you *are* a thief then? A common criminal?" he said.

"Well, don't say it like that," whined Azron. "You make it sound like I'm some sort of bad person!"

"Well, yes, that's the point!" said Bip.

Azron chuckled under his breath. "Of course. I keep forgetting you're not from around here. Look, the way we do things in Port Town is a bit different from other places. Now how can I put this?" Azron frowned into space for a moment. "Well, put it like this," he continued. "We don't really have much of a currency, yeah? We just trade commodities as they are, usually, and that's fine if you've got commodities to begin with, see? But some people don't, so they trade services, yeah? But the whole process, it's a bit slow, isn't it? So what people do, right, is they, like, cut out the middle man?" Azron peered hopefully at Bip to see if he was following.

"Are you trying to tell me," said Bip, slowly. "That everybody steals from everybody else?"

"Exactly!" said Azron, grinning hugely. "Obviously, there's legitimate trade on some levels, but only when it can't be avoided."

"But why?" cried Bip in hopeless confusion.

"Less paperwork, less bureaucracy, less class division, less unemployment. It works on a lot of levels, really," said Azron.

"But it's completely lawless!" wailed Bip.

"Of course it's not! Violent crime isn't tolerated, for a start. And then there's the law of Fair Cop, which means if you get caught nicking, you've got to give everything back. And the government steals taxes, instead of threatening people for them…" Azron stopped as he took in Bip's look of horrified confusion. "I'll tell you what," he said. "Why don't you just wait until we get there?"

PORT TOWN WAS A MESS. A beautiful chaos of noise and activity, a profound ugliness of cramped buildings and surging crowds. Squat houses of badly cut brick and wood were piled carelessly on top of one another, and the smell of a million people with better things to think about than adequate means of sanitation constantly flicked the nose.

Bip reeled. The quietness of Kaneq was all he had ever known of civilization. The sheer number of people going about their everyday business on an average morning in Port Town made the Apprentice Fair and the yearly carnival of Kaneq seem like a hermit's house party by comparison.

He had first viewed Port Town from a distance when they had crested a large hill, and for a while, he had thought that they had been turned around and were back at the ocean. A huge lake dominated the landscape. Called the Filter by the locals, the lake was the point where nearly every major river in the Free Countries converged before heading out to sea in three giant fingers. Port Town had taken full advantage of this geological oddity and a veritable floating city of docks, harbors, jetties, and ships stretched for miles across the Filter. Not a spare inch wasn't taken up by cargo, cranes, carts, barges, and bridges and, running like ants throughout the complex, hundreds of men and women of various creeds and colors all shouted very loudly at one another. Azron had wisely taken Bip around the dock areas and through the city gates reserved for wagon trade.

Bip had gawked moronically as they had wandered through the muddy, labyrinthine streets. "Busy" was too small a word to sum up the plethora of different activities running across the Port Town streets. Taxis taxied, whores whored, beggars begged, and merchants shouted endlessly. What Bip didn't notice, of course, running like an underlying plot to the entire scene, was the thieves thieving. If he had noticed the sheer amount of swindling, sidling, and just plain swiping that was visible to the trained eye, he probably would have broken down in tears.

"Welcome to Port Town!" said Azron, grinning his lopsided grin and deeply breathing in the bumptious air. "Where do you want to go first?"

Bip took in the hectic scenery with the awestruck terror of a fish that has just jumped out of its bowl and into an ocean. "Can we go somewhere quiet?" he said.

"What?"

"Somewhere quiet! Where I can think for a bit!"

"Quiet?"

"Yes! Quiet!"

Azron thought for a moment. Quiet was a rare adjective in Port Town, but there were places with less noise than others.

"Follow me!" he shouted as he began pushing his way through the crowded streets. Bip followed, wide-eyed and clutching the brim of his traveling hat around his ears to drown out the noise of a lot of people with a lot on their mind.

Bip completely failed to notice, as Azron flowed easily through the crowd, the number of people who would suddenly and frantically pat their pockets soon after brushing against him. A chorus of curses followed the progress of the traveler and the thief.

13

Of Mugs and Minotaurs

They called it the Boiling Sea, though its temperature was, if anything, cold. The word "boiling" referred to the way the waves rose and fell with rapid violence. Even from the very top of the Barrier Cliffs, the turbulent ocean below still loomed menacingly, waves rising and bursting from base to tip of the two-hundred-foot cliff face, hurling thunderous crashes and rainstorms of sea spray against the rocky land.

As far as the eye could see, the waves of the Boiling Sea tossed manically into the sky, each tide a mini-tsunami.

The reason for this was the underwater hurricane, as old as the ocean itself, that raged continuously on the unreachable seabed at the water's center. Unseen in all but its effects, the freak underwater storm made the stretch of sea between the mainland and the new continent a permanent tempest, worthy of the most boisterous of weather demons.

An old woman sat at the cliff's edge, a leather-hooded raincoat obscuring most of her features and an old fishing net in her hand. She dangled her booted feet over the raging waters beneath her and whistled a merry tune against the constant boom of waves smashing against the Barrier Cliffs.

She was fishing for panic fish, one of the few life forms that could survive in the Boiling Sea. The panic fish was a white, oblong creature with extremely small fins. Its inadequacy in the fin department was never really a problem as the panic fish didn't actually swim, it just spent its entire life being thrown through the air by the violence of the Boiling Sea. Living entirely on plankton, which it gorged on in the few moments that it spent in the water, the panic fish led a short and terrifying existence, looking forward only to the time when it might be left in the sea for long enough to reproduce. The panic fish had no natural predators. Unless you counted gravity and stress-related heart failure.

The old lady enjoyed fishing at the Boiling Sea because all you had to do was wait for the hurtling fish to land in your net. She hummed a merry ditty while a panic fish flew through the air nearby emitting a high-pitched keening sound.

She did not see the stranger approach until he was standing next to her. She looked up from her net and took in the newcomer's appearance. For a moment, she thought he might be a pirate or a highwayman, but something in the man's stance and expression said differently. He had the look of someone who was in the middle of running a marathon.

"Help thee, squire?" said the woman.

"What is this?" said the man, gesturing to the chaotic panorama before him.

"Boiling Sea," said the woman. "Pretty, ain't it?" She cackled.

"Does the storm ever stop?" said the newcomer.

"Not in our life time, nay," said the woman. "Boiling Sea is always like this. Never stops."

The man looked out for a while, thinking.

"There's no way across?" he said.

"Not by boat, not unless yer mad or yer not fond of livin'."

"Another way, then?"

"To the mainland?" The old woman spat. "Only way across is the Spine Islands, and they is crawling with monsters so they is. Crossed meself when I was youngun. Came with a caravan of hundreds, arrived with less than half. No place for one man to travel."

The man stood thinking again, surveying the stormy horizon.

"Which way?" he said finally.

The old woman pointed a bony finger to the east. "That way," she muttered. "But I wouldn't bother if I was thee."

The man raised an eyebrow questioningly.

"Why dost thou think people risk life and limb to get to the new continent? Why dost thou think we live hard as pioneers?" said the woman.

The man stared at the old woman for a moment. He had considered this question himself.

"There's nothing back at the mainland but war and death!" said the woman. "And always will be while a Draegul sits on the throne."

The man nodded his head and walked east. The sad truth, he knew, was that wherever there was war and death, civilization was likely to be nearby.

"Nothing but death!" called the old lady, her withered screech rising above the crash of the waves. Handen carried on walking. Death, for him, had ceased to be a problem.

"Glad 'e's gone," muttered the old lady as Handen Strike disappeared out of sight. "'e was scaring the fish anyway."

As if to contest the point, a screaming panic fish went whooping over her head.

CLAMOR HAD TUNED down to commotion. The inside of the Weasel's Face tavern and inn, even though crowded with drunks and braggarts, was still far quieter than the streets outside.

Bip sat in a dark booth in the corner of the inn, his rucksack and traveling hat propped next to him as he waited for Azron to return from the bar. As comfortable as the booth was, Bip was finding it difficult to relax. All his wilderness training now seemed like a waste of time in the face of the thriving Port Town populace. The sheer number of people milling around still unnerved him, and he felt like exactly what he was—a stranger in a strange place.

Azron returned with two foamy mugs of something potent and sat down opposite Bip, sliding one of the glass mugs toward him. Bip looked at it suspiciously.

"How did you pay for this?" he said.

Azron rolled his eyes. "Let's not get into that again, ay?" he said, completely failing to mention that the table behind them was two drinks lighter than it ought to be. Bip shrugged and tried some of the ale. It was pleasant and frothy with a sharp aftertaste.

"So let's hear it, then," said Azron. "I've told you about me—now what's your story?"

Bip thought for a while, sloshing the ale around in his mouth while trying to decide how much information he should divulge to Azron. Finally, not seeing what harm it could do, Bip decided to tell the whole truth. "Well, it turns out I'm descended from an alien race who crash landed here nearly a thousand years ago while they were trying to warn us about an impending disaster that will result in the end of the world and the destruction of the planet some time at the end of this year. I've been sent to warn people." Bip sat back and took another swig of his ale while Azron sat open-mouthed.

"Okay," said Azron after a while. "You're crazy. That's fine. I've worked with crazy people before. Everything's okay."

"I'm not crazy," said Bip in a pained tone of voice. "I'm telling the truth!"

"Yeah, I'm not saying you ain't. It probably is the truth in whatever weird and crazy world your mind resides in. I'm not saying you're a liar, just that you're mental, that's all."

"I'm not mental!" said Bip.

"Yeah, okay, you're not mental. You're the boss, you're the one paying the wages, if you say you're not mental, then that's fine."

"Are you humoring me?" said Bip.

"Would you like me to?" Azron replied.

Bip sighed and put his head in his hands. "Regardless of whether you believe me or not, the world really is going to end, and I need to get to the Empire to warn whoever is in charge."

Azron jumped slightly in his seat and looked sharply around the room.

"What did I tell you about talking loose about the Empire?" he hissed.

"What? What did I say?" said Bip.

"Look," said Azron, leaning in conspiratorially, "the Free Countries and the Empire, yeah? We're not exactly friendly at the minute, see? A lot of personal feelings floating about concerning the Empire and tempers are known to fray, if you get my drift?"

Bip nodded, letting Azron continue.

"You see, the Empire runs half the world, yeah? And those bits it doesn't run…well, let's just say they know what side their bread is buttered on. But the Free Countries, because we've always been a difficult continent to get to, we've always led a fairly independent existence. Though we're officially affiliated with the Empire, we've always adopted the philosophy that what they don't know won't hurt them, sort of thing." Azron paused to drain his mug. He belched loudly before continuing. "But that all changed about fifty years ago when the Empire invented the airboats. Now they've got an airdock in nearly every city in the world and can come and go whenever they please."

"So?" said Bip.

"Well, no one likes it when the landlord turns up, do they? Especially if you haven't paid your rent in about a thousand years. The Empire doesn't like the way the Free Countries are doing things, so every year they send in more troops to keep an eye on things. You didn't hear this from me, right, but if it the Empire keeps on trying to change things around here, there's going to be a war."

"A war?" said Bip.

"Shh! Keep your bloody voice down!" said Azron, waving his hand in frantic gestures. "There's spies all over the place these days—you never know who's listening!"

Bip looked around the tavern. By the bar, an old man was violently sick, and a young serving girl had the misfortune to slip in the result, spilling a tray-load of glasses. He doubted whether anyone was paying attention to his dark little corner.

"Look," said Bip, "my mission is to relay my warning to the most influential person I can find, and as far as I've heard, whoever is in charge of this Empire is the man to speak to, yes?"

"I suppose," said Azron, guardedly.

"So can you get me to see the Emperor?"

Azron cracked his lazy half-smile. "Nobody just *sees* Draegul, mate. You have to be top brass just to get in his vicinity."

"Well, can you at least get me to the Empire?" said Bip.

Azron thought for a moment. "You want to get to the Empire fast, yeah? And the only way you can do that is by airboat to Regalious. You'd need to apply for a ticket and that can take anything up to a year if you're not in the know. Which you're not."

"A year?" wailed Bip.

"Well, they're hardly going to let any old chump into the Empire's mainland, are they? They've got security procedures longer than a jabberwocky's long bits."

"But I need to get there as soon as possible! The world won't even be here in a year!"

"All right, all right!" said Azron. "There is another way. I can probably get you a ticket no problem from the black market...but it'll cost a lot."

Bip pulled the lump of gold from his pocket and dumped it on the table. It made a satisfying clonking noise that made the beer mugs rattle.

"Will that be enough, do you think?" said Bip.

"Great holy bastards!" croaked Azron. "Put that back in your pocket before you get us all killed!"

Azron waited, his brow sweating as he shot panicked glances around the room, carefully making calculations while Bip concealed the fist-sized lump of gold.

"Okay, okay," said Azron, still breathing shallowly. "We'll make some enquiries at the market, but for now, I suggest we get the hell out here before one of the seventeen people who saw that monstrous lump of cash decides they fancy their chances."

Walking hurriedly, the two exited the Weasel's Face. Seventeen pairs of eyes followed them. Several people made their excuses and went out of the back door. None of them looked like particularly friendly people.

The traveler and the thief ducked out of the pub and into the marketplace, which still throbbed with the pulse of extreme commerce. The din of a thousand salesmen jumbled into one cacophony of advertisement. Goods and moneys changed hands quicker than the cards of a street illusionist. And all the while, the thieves jumped in and out of one another's stalls like adulterers in a camp comedy.

Bip steeled himself against the now-familiar sense of agoraphobia, resisting the urge to hang on to Azron's coat as the thief led him through the huddled crowds. Eventually they made their way to a more deserted part of the market, a small clearing decked with shady-looking stalls that backed onto an ominous network of alleyways. Even in the brightness of the afternoon, this particular clearing purveyed the intimacy of midnight.

"You stay here," said Azron, pushing Bip up against a wall. "And for god's sake, don't talk to anyone and keep your things where you can see them!"

"Where are you going?" asked Bip.

"I'm off to see a man about a dog," said Azron mysteriously, before sidling off into an alleyway.

"I should think we've got other things to worry about than pet problems," grumbled Bip to himself. "Only the end of the bloody world..."

He stood against the wall and looked about the marketplace, clutching his bag to his chest while trying to keep a hand on Brian's pommel. His gaze flitted nervously from side to side. Basically, he had the word "tourist" written all over him in large black capitals. Eventually he relaxed and meandered over to one of the many market stalls, gazing dumbly at the various wares while he waited for Azron. The stall keeper, a stout man with hooded eyes, gave Bip an appraising look. Before long, a wide, clean and above all *predatory* grin split his face.

"Welcome stranger!" said the stall-keeper, waving his hand with a flourish. "Welcome to Honest Achmed's Emporium of Antiquities and Distinctive Curiosities!"

Bip blinked, stupidly.

"My stall," said Achmed, helpfully. He leaned over and muttered to Bip conspiratorially, "Am I right in thinking that you're not originally from Port Town?"

"Actually, this is my first time in a city," said Bip, painting a large bullseye on his chest.

"Then you'll want souvenirs, won't you?" said Achmed. "Something to remind you of your visit?" The man began rummaging around on his stall, searching for an appropriate item. Finally, he lifted a rock triumphantly before Bip's nose.

"How about this little beauty, then?" he said.

"It's a rock," stated Bip, more confused than nonplussed.

"Not just a rock, stranger. What I hold in my hand is a piece of history!"

Bip squinted through his glasses. "It looks like a rock to me," he concluded.

"Ah," said Achmed, "but this is the very rock used to assassinate the Trade King in the war of the Six Rivers. This rock has been passed down through the generations as a symbol of the fight for free enterprise against tyrannical business unions! Only three spondulicks and its yours!"

"Sounds fascinating," said Bip, who had no clue what Achmed was on about.

"Not your cup of tea, then?" said the stall-keeper, tossing the rock over his shoulder. "Then how about this?"

"That looks like another rock..."

"Ah!" said Achmed. "It may look like a rock, but it's actually the fossilized remains of the toenail of the giant flying lizards that used to stalk the world at the dawn of history! Yours for only two spondulicks!"

"I don't think so..." said Bip.

"Fair enough, stranger, fair enough... But maybe I can interest you in...this!"

"Now, that," said Bip, "that is an empty jar you just picked up off of the floor."

"Ah!" said Achmed. "It may look like an empty jar I just picked up off of the floor, but it's actually... It's actually... It's actually a jar of invisible face paint!" The stall-keeper held up the jar triumphantly, a smug grin on his face. "Only three spondulicks!"

"Invisible face paint?"

"Yes! You'll be the life of the party if you go back to your friends dressed up in invisible face paint!"

"How will they know I'm wearing it?"

"Well, that's the beauty of it!" said Achmed. "They won't know until you tell them! Imagine their surprise and delight! Only two spondulicks!"

"Are you're sure that's not just an empty jar?"

"Of course not! Would Honest Achmed lie to you? Only one spondulick and it's yours."

At that moment, and luckily for Bip, Azron emerged from the alleyways with a mildly annoyed expression on his usually smirking features.

"Clear off, Bare-Face, this mug is mine," he snarled, prodding the merchant in the face with one of his long, delicate fingers.

"Who's Bare-Face?" said Bip.

"He is," said Azron, nodding to the greasy salesman. "He's Achmed D'lyer, one of the biggest codswallopers this side of the docks!"

"But he told me his name was Honest Achmed!" said Bip.

"Well, that's the things about liars, see? They tend to bend the truth a bit," said Azron.

"Well, if everything's in order here, it really is time for me to close up," said Achmed, backing away surreptitiously.

"Not so fast," said Azron. He turned to Bip. "Did you buy anything from this man?" he demanded.

"Well, I was tempted by the invisible face paint…" said Bip.

Azron clucked and rolled his eyes before turning around and giving Achmed's stall a swift kick. "Go and hock your dodgy goods elsewhere, you con man! Honestly, you give thievery a bad name!" The stall-keeper grinned, shrugged, and turned back to his wares. Azron shook his head disapprovingly. "You should really be more careful, mate," he said, turning back to Bip. "There's all sorts around these parts."

"He seemed all right," said Bip reproachfully.

The thief just clucked and rolled his eyes again. "If you want to survive in this town, mate, you've got to realize there are two types of people: mugs and muggers. The trick is not to be the mug. Now, come on, follow me."

They began walking through the alleyways of Port Town, Azron's gaze shifting constantly from shadow to shadow.

"So, did you find out about the airboat ticket?" said Bip.

"Everyone's tight-lipped," said Azron. "They're all too scared of Argustin spies around here, so it looks like we're going to have to trade with the goblins. They can get their hands on anything."

"Goblins?" said Bip.

"King Chaff's tribe. They live outside the city. They're a traveling community, so they don't really care much about the Empire."

"Are goblins trustworthy?" Bip asked.

"No," replied Azron. "And that's exactly why we're approaching them for a highly illegal black-market airboat ticket, guv. It's not the sort of thing I'd ask a policeman for now, is it?"

"'Spose not," mumbled Bip.

"Now," said Azron, "if I could have a bit of quiet, please, I'll see if I can get us through these alleyways without being robbed or stabbed, shall I?"

While Azron was talking, he turned a corner and walked straight into five knife-wielding robbers.

"Nice try," said Bip.

"Oh, crap."

Mug or mugger. Dinner or diner. Bip was beginning to realize that maybe the wilds and the city had something in common after all. They were both full of predators.

KEROS THE MINOTAUR stomped around the village square, raising dust under his cloven feet and swinging his humungous club in wide arcs around his horned head. He bellowed ferociously as the scattering villagers fled to the relative safety of their houses. Very few people would stick around in the presence of an angry minotaur, a monster that was half man, half bull, and wholly unpleasant.

With one final roar, Keros stopped stomping around and leaned his massive frame casually on his club. All the villagers had fled. They would be back, the minotaur knew, with sacrificial livestock, barrels of ale, and with any luck, a few youngest daughters.

The life of a minotaur was an easy one, consisting mainly of traveling from village to village, killing any of the men-folk stupid enough to stand in his way, then roaring menacingly until the villagers got the hint and started giving him presents. Keros looked down at the corpse of the village's most recent champion. It hadn't been much of a challenge, a young man barely out of his teens carrying a home-cast sword he had wielded inexpertly. The creature snorted through his bull's nose. Maybe he would leave off the villages for a while and give them time to build up their numbers again. After all, there was no sense in scaring off such lucrative benefactors.

The monster was interrupted in his thoughts by a piercing whistle from behind him. He turned to face the intruder, half expecting some last-minute resistance from the villagers. Instead, he was presented with a single man, silhouetted against the setting sun. Keros had faced many champions before, but something about the stance of the newcomer was unsettling. Perhaps it was the way he hadn't even drawn his weapons yet. Normally at this point, the minotaur would begin roaring and swinging his club, but something told him that the newcomer would not be so easily intimidated.

"Oo argh yoo?" Keros bellowed.

The figure began a slow approach. "For what it's worth, my name is Handen Strike. I doubt you'll be alive long enough to tell anyone."

The minotaur roared with guttural laughter. "Oo challange me?" he said.

"Not much of a challenge," replied Handen stoically.

Keros screamed with rage and lowered his massive head and charged, the ground shaking under the pounding of his hooves. At the last minute before impact with the awaiting Handen, the charging monster leaped into the air, twisting his massive frame and bringing the club down with a blow that cracked the earth beneath it.

Those who had watched the fight from the safety of their houses would later recount that they were sure the stranger had been killed, that there was no way on Bersch he could possibly have avoided the blow. But nevertheless, one moment Handen was directly under the descending doom of the minotaur's club, the next he was simply five feet back and watching the confused beast with a cynical smirk on his face.

Before Keros could regain his composure, Handen sprinted lightly up the creature's club and sprang into the air, kicking the beast hard in the face as he flew overhead. Handen had landed, rolled to his feet, and drawn his weapons before his opponent had even realized what had happened.

The minotaur turned around, snorting hot, wet air from his nostrils, shocked fury blazing in his eyes. "Oo 'ill die slo!" he roared.

Handen cracked his whip. "No," he said. "I really don't think so."

Blinded by anger, the beast lowered his head, readying his dull but powerful horns, and charged again. This time Handen rolled sideways, allowing the speeding minotaur to skid past him before flicking his whip out and wrapping it around the monster's throat. Fighting for breath, Keros bucked and pulled and finally yanked at the whip hard enough to jerk Handen high into the air. Rather than losing his advantage, as Keros had hoped, Handen embraced the momentum of his flight, flourishing his sword in mid-air before landing the blade in the nape of the minotaur's neck with a downward thrust. Keros stopped bucking and collapsed to the floor with a thud. He was dead before he hit the ground.

Handen stood over the fallen monster, his face impassive as he wound his whip back and retrieved his sword. Slowly, the villagers returned from their houses, silent with awe.

The village patriarch approached. "Sire, you have slain the minotaur! Truly thou art a warrior of heroic proportions!"

"Yeah," said Handen. "I get that a lot, actually."

The villagers looked at one another, waiting for the first person to shout "hooray" so that they could join in without looking foolish.

"Our gratitude is bottomless, sire. Ask what you will, and we shall provide!"

"Well, if you could give me directions to the Spine Islands, that would be good," said Handen. "I'm a little lost."

The Patriarch blinked. "I can point thee in the right direction, sire, but the way is fraught with peril, monsters of—"

"Yeah, yeah. Terrible monsters, sinister pirates, and things that no mortal man should ever see. I got the message from the last village elder. Which way, please?"

The Patriarch pointed the direction. "Did he mention the terrible evils of the—"

"Of the Bat Cult, yes. And the Snake Cult and the Snail Cult, also."

"Ah, but did he tell thee of the—"

"Shadow Beast of Bogmon Swamp? Yeah, yeah."

"But what of—"

"The Unholy Armies of the Ever Living Skelera. Yep, he filled me in on that as well."

The Patriarch tried not to look disappointed. "Oh. Well. I suppose you should get off, then. Just keep going southeast. You can't miss them."

"Yeah, thanks, bye."

The villagers watched as the hero walked off into the sunset.

"Seemed like a nice enough chap," one remarked.

"Yeah. So. What do we do now, then?" said another.

"Well, I was saving this barrel of ale for the minotaur, but I suppose that's out of the window now, isn't it?"

"Yeah. Sort of don't know what to do with myself now. I had the rest of the evening booked to complain about the minotaur."

"Well, I for one," said somebody's youngest daughter, "am very grateful things have worked out this way. I think a celebration is in order. In honor of the brave man who saved us from the tyrannies of the minotaur."

"Yeah, great!"

"Yeah!"

"Brilliant!"

"What did he say his name was?"

"I dunno. I'm not letting this barrel go to waste, though."

"Brilliant!"

BIP AND AZRON backed away from the muggers. They were almost archetypal muggers, bulky and scarred with a malignant glee in their eye that one normally associated with playground brawlers.

"All right then, lads, what do you want?" said Azron, though he had already guessed the answer.

The lead mugger, bearing more scars and bulk than his comrades, flicked his dagger from hand to hand in an absent-minded kind of way. "We want what 'e's got in 'is pocket," he sneered, nodding toward Bip.

Bip rummaged around in his pocket for a while before producing a half-eaten corned beef sandwich. "This?" he suggested, hopefully.

Azron rolled his eyes. "I think perhaps they're referring to the huge lump of gold you were flaunting recklessly in the pub earlier, mate."

"Bingo!" said the head mugger.

Bip leaned toward Azron. "What's bingo?" he whispered.

"It's a game played by old ladies."

"Well what's that go to do with—"

"Never mind. What he's trying to say is, he wants your lump of gold."

"Well he can't have it," said Bip matter-of-factly. "I need it."

Azron looked at the five wickedly sharp daggers pointing in their direction. "You tell them that. I don't think they'll listen, mate."

"Sorry, chaps," said Bip, in a sincerely apologetic tone, "but I really need this lump of gold. It's the only one I have, you see? So you can't have it."

Azron smacked his hand over his eyes in horror and embarrassment. The muggers looked at one another in amused confusion.

"I think it's possible you don't fully understand the situation you're in, boy," said the mugger prime. "You either give us the gold or we stab you until you die. Or if you prefer the classic terminology, your money or your life. Understand?"

"Ah," said Bip. "Then I'm afraid you leave me no choice." With a sound like silk committing suicide, Bip drew Brian from his scabbard, flourishing the thin blade before him in the defensive stance he had been taught by Rynford.

Azron groaned heavily. "Are you mental?" he muttered.

"I thought you'd already made up your mind about that?" said Bip.

"Well, yeah, I knew you were mental but not *mental* mental. There's five of them and one of you. You don't stand a chance."

"He's right, you know," said one of the muggers helpfully.

Bip flourished his sword, spinning it around his head in a way he hoped looked vaguely masterful. "Yes, well. Did I mention I've been trained intensively by the finest Huntmaster of Kaneq?"

"No," said the lead mugger indifferently. "Now prepare to die slowly and painfully."

"Ah," said Bip, backing away from the advancing muggers. "That didn't go exactly as I planned."

"You tit," said Azron. "You complete and utter tit. You could have just given them the gold, but no, now we have to die. Nice one, mate, you're a real joy to be around."

"I was sort of hoping I could sort of bluff them," replied Bip. "It doesn't look like they're easily intimidated."

"No. You see large groups of thugs with knives rarely are intimidated. Especially by some kid with arms like twigs and a sword that looks like it was made for opening letters!"

"Well, there's no need to be rude about it," said Bip, reproachfully.

"We are going to die!" cried Azron. "I'll be as rude as I bloody well please!"

The thief and the traveler backed into a wall, cutting off any hope of escape. Much worse than being caught between a rock and a hard place, they were caught between a solid brick wall and several angry people with sharp implements. The muggers advanced with a horrible casualness, murder quite clearly shining in their eyes.

Bip thought quickly, his mind racing as he tried to remember his training. *What would Rynford do?* he thought to himself. *Probably something impressively acrobatic, then beat everyone to death with a stick. And then eat them, probably...*

Bip looked at the muggers, each of them at least twice as broad as he was. He might be able to fight one of them, but five was beyond the reaches of reason. This left Bip with only one real option—psyence.

Sheathing Brian back in his scabbard, Bip calmed his mind and tried to concentrate on the Fire Dance. The words of Glimton's teachings came back to him.

You must calm your mind, be at one with your surroundings. Silence the voice in your head.

I said SILENCE IT, you pleb!

His mind fully focused, Bip concentrated.

Concentrated...

14

Goblins in Designer Jeans

Azron and Bip sat in the wagon they had "commandeered" from outside a shop back in Port Town. The city sprawled in the distance behind them as they made their way out to the grassy plains, pulled by a sturdy donkey with a *laissez faire* approach to life. They were on their way to see the goblins and were, so far, making good progress on the barely beaten track.

"That was good, that was, mate," said Azron, reflectively.

"I told you I don't want to talk about it," replied Bip.

"Yeah, but the way your hat just exploded like that…"

"Shut up."

"It was really impressive."

The wagon trundled along in the quiet afternoon. Somewhere a pigeon made a pigeon noise.

"And, of course, it scared the absolute crap out of those muggers," said Azron, eventually.

"Shh," said Bip.

"I've never seen grown men run so fast. Anyone would think they hadn't seen a chap's hat explode violently for no apparent reason before."

"…" said Bip.

"Shame, though," said Azron. "It was a nice hat."

Bip nodded his agreement. His traveling hat, which had contained many useful provisions, had been blown into smithereens when his latest psyentific escapade had gone massively askew. He had intended to scare off the muggers, granted, but exploding his hat had not been part of his plan.

"So how did you do it, then? Explode your hat, I mean? Magic, was it?" said Azron.

Bip frowned briefly, not recognizing the term. "It was psyence," he muttered.

"What, like chemicals and things?"

"Sort of," said Bip. "It's an innate ability to empathize with and persuade the energy fields and physical equations of objects on a molecular level."

"Ah, really? Thought as much," said Azron.

The wagon rolled along for a while, one of its axels squeaking with a chirpy rhythm.

"So what did all those words you just said mean, exactly?" said Azron.

"Well, in my case, it means I can explode things just by thinking about it," replied Bip.

"Sounds...useful?" said Azron.

"Oh yes," said Bip glumly. "The only drawback being that, more often than not, I don't actually want things to explode."

"So that hat thing...that was an accident?"

"In a word, yes. I had actually intended to launch a wave of fire at our assailants. Unfortunately, for reasons beyond me, I exploded my hat instead."

The wagon rolled along. Azron tried hard to conceal a smirk.

"So," he said, "do you always explode things when you don't mean to?"

"No," said Bip. "Sometimes I turn them into igloos. I can do igloos."

"Oh," said Azron. "Handy, I suppose..."

"Oh, yes. If you want something exploded or turned into an igloo, I'm the chap to talk to," said Bip.

"I'll bear that in mind."

Suddenly an arrow zipped through the air and thunked into the front of the wagon, narrowly missing Bip's knee.

"Looks like we're here," said Azron.

THE GOBLINS WERE AN UNUSUAL SPECIES–NOT quite human and not quite monster. They were often thin-limbed and spindly, with skin so pale it would hue into a faint green or blue. Their noses were uniformly bulbous, and their ears pointed far over the crests of their heads, which were cue-ball bald bar a tuft that grew at the very back of their craniums. This tuft was often grown as long as possible and plaited intricately, particularly with the females.

Though diminutive in stature, the goblins possessed a wiry strength and an innate viciousness. Their teeth grew to neat, foxlike points, and much of their skin was adorned with tattoos and body-piercings. The weapons they carried were crude, home-made affairs. Though, as Bip was quickly finding out, when someone points a bow and arrow at your face, quality of craftsmanship ceases to be a pressing concern.

"Whatyewantin?" said one of the three goblins that surrounded the wagon, its voice clipped and harsh.

"All right, chum?" said Azron, raising his hands to show he was unarmed, then fishing out his union certificate, showing it as a policeman might show a badge. "Come to talk to the big cheese, haven't I? King Chaff about, is he?"

"Yegotanappointmentthereboyo? said the goblin.

"No?" said Azron.

"S'alrightyedinnineedone," said the goblin. "Comeonthenwhatye-waitingfer? Writtneinvitation?" With that, the three goblins stomped off into the nearby woodland. Azron flicked the reins of the wagon and provoked the donkey into a slow trot. They began to follow the goblins.

"Did you understand a word of that?" said Bip, looking bewildered.

"Oh yeah, they speak good enough Imperial," said Azron. "They just speak very quickly. It's designed to throw people off when they're bargaining, see?"

The goblins strolled through the woodland at a casual pace verging on a saunter, while the wagon trundled easily behind. Eventually, the woodland cleared into a scrubby clearing where a large cluster of shoddily constructed caravans and animal-skin tents marked the current territory of the goblin tribe.

Many goblin children ran around shrieking aimlessly, dressed in dungarees or, seemingly, whatever clothes they had found lying around. Older goblins sat playing one-up on rickety tables, dressed in shiny suits that had probably fitted their original owners quite well. Here and there goblin women busied themselves seeing to the chores, which seemed to consist entirely of hitting their children with sticks until the chores were done.

The vibrancy and ruckus of King Chaff's tribal community came to a dead stop as the wagon pulled into the clearing. Every goblin man, woman, and child froze immediately, fixing the newcomers with mixed expressions of mistrust and appraisal. Then, almost as if they had never stopped, the goblins continued about their business with masterful nonchalance, only occasionally casting quick, beady glances over their shoulders at the strangers.

Something that struck Bip immediately was the amount of gold present around the campsite. Every goblin in view, from the smallest toddler to the frailest old man, was adorned with all manner of large and gaudy golden jewelry. From rings to necklaces, bracelets and earrings, every goblin seemed dressed up with more gold than Bip had ever seen in one place, let alone on one person. Without thinking, he nervously clutched at the gold nugget in his pocket.

"Don't worry about it," said Azron, leaning over conspiratorially. "It's not real gold they're wearing. They would have traded it ages ago if it was. It's only fake jewelry. It's a bit of a status symbol in goblin communities. They call it 'bling.' It's all for show, see?"

One of the escorts returned. "Y'alrighttherepal? Bigy-in'llseeyeznow."

Bip and Azron stepped from the wagon and followed the escort to the largest of the caravans. Outside the door, two goblins serving as guards made a halfhearted show of vigilance. They made a point of glaring suspiciously at the newcomers for a while before they grudgingly waved them into the caravan.

The first thing Bip noticed as he entered the caravan was the smell, a dried in tang of mushroom and spice. It put him in mind of spoiled food and damp carpet. As his eyes adjusted to the gloom, what he had first assumed to be a mound of cushions gradually revealed its self to be a goblin of massive proportions. It was immediately clear that this was King Chaff, the goblin "Big Cheese". For a start he was so fat his shape gave the general impression of a water balloon with legs. The obese creature sat propped against a huge, overstuffed armchair and his body was adorned with more bling than Bip could have ever thought possible. Between the weight of his excess fat and the weight of his jewelry, Bip was surprised that King Chaff did not fall right though the floor of his caravan.

"Howyez," said the goblin king, his voice husky and slower than his comrades.

"All right, Mr. King?" said Azron, bowing low and motioning for Bip to do the same. As Bip bowed, he noticed an assorted pile of rotting animal bones at the King's feet, like a particularly revolting pouffe.

"YeztradingItakeit?" said the king. He pulled, from some unknown crevice, a large joint of greasy chicken, which he began to chomp on methodically. Bip tried to ignore the flip-flop sensation in his stomach. Watching the goblin eat was an experience he would try hard to forget.

"As a matter of fact, Your Largeness, yes, we are," replied Azron.

"Whatyezwant?" said King Chaff, chicken juice running down his many chins.

"We need airboat tickets to the mainland," said Azron.

The king paused mid-mastication and looked hard at Azron. For a moment, Bip thought the large goblin was simply going to laugh out loud, and part of him hoped that he would—the malodorous caravan and the king's upsetting eating habits were giving Bip a strong desire for fresher air. Instead, the king swallowed and said, "Naybother. Whatchoogotferme?"

Azron nudged Bip, who took the large lump of gold from his pocket. Even in the murkiness of the caravan, the nugget gleamed with an alluring light.

"Muchobling," gasped King Chaff.

"Yes indeedy," said the thief.

The fat goblin composed himself, his many chins wobbling as he shook his head. "Gizamotothinkaboutitwillye?" he said.

"Certainly, Your Obesity," said Azron. "We'll be outside, yeah?"

BIP SAT on the wagon watching a goblin child poke the donkey with a stick, an attitude of near-furious concentration on its face. The donkey took the aggressive curiosity with the same placid indifference as it took almost everything that life threw at it. Azron lay back in the weak sunshine, idly chewing on a piece of long grass.

"He seemed pretty impressed," said Bip after a while. "Do you think he'll trade the airboat tickets for the gold?"

"I shouldn't think so," said Azron. "Goblins hardly ever trade in cash."

"What? Then why did we even bother showing him it?" said Bip.

"I told you already, they respect bling. He probably wouldn't even consider trading with us if we didn't have a sufficient amount of bling about our persons."

"Then what will he want in exchange?" said Bip.

"Who knows?" said Azron, lazily. "It's difficult to tell. Could be they want a herd of cattle. Could be they want the still-beating heart of one of their enemies. Always a surprise when you deal with goblins."

Bip swallowed hard.

"Heymisterz!" The escort from earlier approached the wagon from across the campsite. "Thebigyin'smadeuphismind.Sezhewantstotrade."

"Nice one!" said Azron. "And what does he want?"

The goblin pulled Azron's coat until the lanky thief's head was level with its mouth and began whispering at length. Bip strained his ears trying to hear what was being said but couldn't. Eventually the goblin wandered off back to the campsite.

"The price has been set," said Azron, his voice flat.

"What do they want?" asked Bip.

"They want clothes," said Azron.

"Clothes? Is that all?"

"Not all. Not all exactly," said Azron. "They want a hundred pairs of designer jeans."

"Oh," said Bip. "And what are they, exactly?"

"Well, they're a form of denim trousers that are popular with construction workers and are now sought after by fashion-conscious men and women with too much time on their hands."

"Well, that doesn't seem too bad…" muttered Bip.

"Are you kidding, mate?" cried Azron. "Some of those jeans can sell for a couple of hundred spondulicks!"

"Why on Bersch would anyone pay that much for a pair of trousers?" said Bip.

"Well, it's like the goblins and their bling, yeah? It's a status symbol thing," explained Azron.

Bip took the lump of gold from his pocket. "Do you think we'll have enough?" he said glumly.

"Well, you would've had," said Azron, "but they want half the nugget as well."

"What?"

"As a gesture of goodwill."

"What?"

"Calm down, calm down! These are black market airboat tickets, mate, they don't grow on trees! There's security papers to be forged, false identities to be made. It all adds up, you know."

Bip sighed heavily. Just as things had seemed to be progressing, he had hit a seemingly insurmountable wall.

"Look, cheer up, mate," said Azron eventually. "This isn't as bad as it looks, yeah?"

"What do you mean?" said Bip.

"Have you forgotten?" Azron grinned. "I'm a Diamond Geezer, mate. First class! I've got contacts, I've got know-how." The thief wiggled his long, delicate digits. "I've got a five-finger discount as long as your arm!"

"You're not suggesting we steal, are you?" gasped Bip.

"Oh, yes, I bloody well am!"

HANDEN APPROACHED the shores of Blood River. It was everything he had expected. Thick mist rolled quietly about the dry reeds, and a wind like an urgent whisper blew through the dark leaves of the trees above. A cold, deathly feeling rolled in off the stock-still waters of the iron-gray river. Far off in the distance, the hazy form of the first of the Spine Islands loomed menacingly.

Handen sighed. He was growing tired of ominously evil locations.

To his left, an ancient horn hung from the branch of a crooked tree with wicked-looking carvings inscribed on its trunk. Handen didn't bother to attempt to translate the carvings; he merely grabbed the horn and blew hard. A sound like a sea-beast in mourning echoed across the grave landscape.

The former Hostilities Advisor waited, tapping his foot impatiently. The journey to the shores of Blood River should only have taken him a couple of months, but for a number of reasons (including damsels in distress, peasant rebellions, monster attacks, evil cults, lost tombs, and more adventures than he could even remember), it had taken him several years. It wasn't that time held much personal meaning for him anymore—and there was plenty of time until the end of the world—it was just that Handen was beginning to feel that the world was against him, that it didn't *want* to be saved. And so, having finally reached the only access point to the Spine Islands, and after summoning the Dread Ferryman of Blood River, Handen fumed quietly at yet another unnecessary delay.

A quiet ripple in the water heralded the approach of the ferry. A shadow began to form in the river mist, gradually revealing a black-cloaked figure on a rickety wooden raft, inching slowly toward the shore.

"What's your problem? Are you paid by the hour or something?" said Handen, when the ferryman had reached the shore.

"Sssilence, mortal," hissed the Dread Ferryman, as red eyes glowed like brimstone in the deep cowl that hid his face in shadow. He lifted a hand from the folds of his cloak to reveal fingers of bone underneath. Handen was unimpressed. He had seen plenty of animated skeletons in the past decade and was no longer surprised by them.

"If the River of Blood you wisssh to crosss, thou must anssswer me a riddle," said the Dread Ferryman.

"Couldn't I just give you some money?" said Handen. "I have money right here, look."

"A riddle," repeated the ferryman.

"Fine, then—tell me your bloody riddle," Handen growled.

The ferryman cleared his throat (though he needn't have bothered, being skeletal and all).

I am three full circles round,
But I am also like a square.
I am like to many things,
Yet nothing can compare.
I am divine as god blood,
I am as pure as snow.
I am unholy water,
I feed the laughing crow.
What am I?"

The ferryman leaned back smugly as Handen frowned in concentration. "Ansswer true," he hissed. "And know that falsssehood meansss your doom."

The adventurer continued to frown into space.

"Like a square yet three full circles round?" he said, after a while.

"Yesss," answered the ferryman.

"As divine as god blood?"

"Yesss."

"You feed the laughing crow?"

"Yesss."

"I believe I have the answer," said Handen.

With an enormous right hook, Handen sent the Dread Ferryman sprawling into the water. Before the creature could fully resurface, Handen jammed a boot down on the top of its skull.

"Now listen to me, you skeletal bastard," he said. "All this riddle crap might work for the tourists, but it doesn't hold water with me, right?"

"You can't say that!" wailed the ferryman.

"Shut up. Here's what's going to happen, right? You're going to give me a lift in your poxy little boat to the other side of this river, or I'm going to smash you into pieces and turn you into scrimshaw, understood?"

"Don't you know who I am?" screeched the skeletal ferryman.

Handen leaned down menacingly. "You know, the Wolf King of Uldale said exactly the same thing to me just before I stabbed him several times in the eye. And the Vampire Maiden of Duxbridge said something similar just before I kicked her into a bonfire. So go ahead, waste more of my time with idiot questions and see just how razor-thin my patience really is!"

The ferryman wisely kept his mandibles shut. He climbed back into the boat with as much dignity as he could muster and, with Handen as his passenger, began wading slowly out toward the Spine Islands.

Handen lay back in the ferry. "And row faster, for god's sake, some of us have got places to be."

He was in no mood for more delays.

BIP WAITED outside the Pig and Thistle Inn, huddled against a wall with an air of justified paranoia. It had been a good five hours since they'd arrived back in Port Town, most of which Bip had spent waiting outside pubs for Azron, who was doing something he called "networking."

So far, "networking" had consisted of getting steadily more drunk and chatting to various people who all looked as seedy as, if not seedier than, Azron himself.

It was dark now in Port Town, and though the streets were still crowded with people and the lamps had been lit at twilight, Bip was nevertheless unnerved by the city at night. He watched the shadows, nervously clutching Brian's hilt, too aware of what an easy target he was.

The Kaneqian nearly jumped out of his skin when Azron tapped him on the shoulder from behind.

"We're on," said Azron.

"What? On what?" said Bip. Then, "What took you so long?"

"Hey! Networking's a delicate business, mate—you've got to be careful who you're talking to. Get the right information without giving too much away, like."

"Well, what did you find out?" asked Bip.

"There's a delivery to Tony Topman's Clothing Shoppe at midnight tonight. A whole stagecoach filled with designer gear and more armed guards than most people can count."

Bip's heart sank. "I suppose robbing the stagecoach is out of the question, then. Will we have to steal from the shop itself?"

"Are you kidding? You don't break into one of Topman's places— the man's a psychopath! Undisputed don of the denim mafia! He's got more thugs on his payroll than I'd care to think about!" said Azron. "It'd be suicide to try to haul a load as large as the one we're after out of one of Topman's places."

"What do we do, then?" said Bip.

Azron grinned his crooked grin. "A good thief never tackles a problem head on. Not when he can go around it."

IT WAS a good living being a guard in Port Town. There was always demand for a decent guard in a place where even the things that were nailed down tended to be lifted. All you needed to be a successful guard was a sharp eye, about eight stone of excess muscle, and a ballistic attitude to anything that came too close to you.

Some of the best hired guards in the whole of Port Town marched in a ring of steel around the slowly advancing stagecoach, crossbows cocked and leveled, ready to fire.

Captain Burney "Easily Aggravated" Dogson sat atop the stagecoach, staring grimly into the shadows around him. Burney and his boys were being paid top whack to move clothing items that had recently become more valuable than gold. He had already had to break the fingers of one of his own men, who had tried to smuggle a netted cravat down his trousers. Burney didn't really understand the appeal of designer clothing, or why some people put such a high value on it, but his was not to reason why, his was but to mash people's fingers with hammers or occasionally shoot them in the face with a crossbow.

The stagecoach pulled up to the trade entrance of Tony Topman's Clothing Shoppe, and Burney jumped down to talk to the two guards who had slithered from the shadows like pictures appearing in an inkblot. They wore the usual attire of Topman's employees—dark hoods and black leather armor, tailored in whatever style was currently deemed to be "in."

"Papers to sign," said Burney, his voice as gruff as his appearance indicated. He held out a clipboard as the taller of the two guards approached. Burney noticed the shorter of the two hanging back. He squinted through the darkness.

"A bit short for a Topman guard, isn't he?" he said.

"I often find that size isn't everything," hissed the taller guard. "In fact, I often find that a couple of inches will suffice." The hooded guard nodded down at the slim and razor-looking dagger that had slid almost magically into his hand.

"Yeah, all right," said Burney. "No need to get shirty. If you just sign the papers, we'll supervise the loading and be on our way."

The Topman guard seemed to hesitate. "We don't need to be supervised," he said.

Burney frowned. "We've orders to make sure everything arrives on the premises safe and sound," he said.

"Orders have changed," said the guard. "Tony doesn't want any non-personnel on his property. We'll take care of the loading."

Burney looked around. He had expected more guards, and frankly, he had expected bigger guards, but he knew you didn't mess around with Tony's boys, who were all hired on the merit of their psychological instability.

"All right then, mate," said Burney. "Our work is done, then. You can tell your boss that we still expect the same pay regardless."

"He will be told," said the guard.

Burney shook his head and walked off back to the stagecoach, where the boxes of designer clothing were being stacked outside the loading gate.

The two sinister guards watched as Burney's men finished unloading and made their way back to their respective homes. Then one of the guards pulled back his hood.

"Well, that was close," said Azron.

15

The Getaway

The Diamond Geezer (1st class) had made it seem like child's play. It had been, as Azron had pointed out, a matter of calling in favors. It turned out that there were a lot of people who owed Azron favors in Port Town.

The first favor he called in had been at Floyd's Pharmacy, where he had obtained several milligrams of something potent and odorless. The next favor had been with the runner boy at Haggie's Coffee House, who frequently received good business from Topman's guards. Then it had simply been a matter of cause and effect.

It had been the work of a minute to drag the drugged security guards out of sight and don the clothing of the smallest two. The rest had been a combination of bluff and luck. All in all, Azron had been pleased with the results. They had loaded up their wagon and made off with the designer gear with hurried nonchalance, ditching the guard uniforms at the earliest opportunity. It had been a cinch to get past the watchmen at the wagon gates, who were so frequently paid to look the other way that they spent most of their time with their noses against a wall.

Now Azron and Bip made their way back to King Chaff's camp across the post-midnight landscape, a fat and generous moon lighting the way, their trusty donkey ambling with all the urgency of a snail with nowhere to go. Azron smoked a victory cigarette, puffing gray clouds into the still night air.

"That went better than I expected," commented Bip.

"Explain," said Azron.

"Well, I thought that there'd be, you know, sneaking about in the shadows and hanging upside down from ceilings," said Bip.

"Nah," said Azron. "All that kerfuffle is for when you want to get something out of somewhere. All we did was stop something getting into somewhere."

"Oh," said Bip, and then after a while, "Still. You made it seem rather easy."

"Easy?" Azron clucked his tongue. "It was years of contacts and wheeling and dealing that allowed me to pull that job off in a hurry. Besides, it's not the doing it that's the hard part. It's the getting away with it."

"How do you mean?"

Azron dragged hard on his dwindling cigarette. "Do you really think it's going to take long for Tony to realize who's nicked his stuff?" he said. "I give it about three hours before he's got every snitch and hired knife in the whole of Port Town looking for me."

"What will you do?"

"Simple," said Azron. "I'm going to go to the Empire with you."

"But you'll need a ticket, surely?" said Bip.

"Already sorted. The deal I came to with King Chaff included two tickets."

Bip thought for a minute. A slow frown began to trickle across his forehead.

"Well, surely that means," he said, "that I could have afforded a single ticket with the money I had?"

"Oh, yes," said Azron, jetting smoke from his nostrils. "But I've always wanted to see Regalious. Things are getting a bit stale in Port Town, to tell you the truth. I want to go where there's more challenging prospects, like."

"You mean to say we just risked life and limb because you fancy a holiday?"

Calm down, mate. I got you your ticket, didn't I?"

"…" said Bip.

"Aw. You haven't gone in a mood with me, have you?" said Azron.

"…" said Bip.

"Cheer up. It could have been worse. Originally, I was planning to drug you, take all your possessions, and sell you to the orcen sailors as a slave."

"What?" screeched Bip.

"Hey! Calm down! I didn't do it, did I?" said Azron.

"Oh, really," huffed Bip sarcastically. "And what made you change your mind? Crisis of conscience?"

"No, don't be silly," said Azron. "Truth is, I like your style. You're a good kid, mate, and that's no lie. You being an out-of-towner and all got me thinking about foreign lands, see? And when you mentioned that you needed to get to the Empire…well, it just sort of inspired me."

Bip huffed and frowned at the floor.

"Besides," said Azron, "if the world really is ending, and you do manage to save it, you can remember your old pal Azron Bezron when it's time for the big fat rewards, yeah?"

PORT TOWN'S airdock was a frenzied affair. So large it warranted its own township, the airdock was home to thousands, whether they be dock-workers, shop-keeps, security, and hospital staff or merely the hundreds of travelers who spent a great deal of time in the soul-pounding limbo of flight delay. The airdock accommodated people from all walks of life.

On the outskirts of the terminals, lines of washing crisscrossed between tall, haphazard buildings, the crowded residential blocks that housed staff and their families. Shops and banks filled the gaps in the streets below, and jugglers and actors wandered throughout, preying on the boredom of the terminal-bound travelers. The terminally bored.

Port Town's airdock, so far, was the only one established in the Free Countries. Consequently, the tide of travelers and goods flowing to and from the Empire was so large that the waiting list to board the few and far between airboats sometimes stretched to months. Port Town's was the only airdock on Bersch to have a family planning clinic.

The main runways and terminals of the airdock resembled normal shipping docks, laden with cargo and great queues of people huddled around the small balloon cranes that hauled people and products to the airboats above. Here and there, impassive staff explained the same things over and over to different red-faced travelers while an atmosphere of condensed headache stung the senses. Rows of uncomfortable chairs held hundreds of refugee-like boarders, all waiting for their departure time. Some, who could not afford accommodation in the area, had taken up camp.

The airboats hung above the port like honey-drunk bees, their large, bulbous hydrosacs swaying gently in the breezy altitude, creaking and swelling like a very fat person in a diving suit. The seemingly unplanned shapes of the dirigibles contrasted oddly with the rigid boxiness of the fuselages that were suspended beneath them, held sure by ropes, chains, and bolts. The airboats had a façade of fragility about them, the very improbability of their flight inviting the mind to consider calamity. It seemed that at any moment they could descend from the sky, their merry buoyancy reclaimed by gravity, their idle dream of flight coming, quite literally, down to earth. It was all too easy to imagine the airboats crashing hugely into the ground below, so delicate their levitation seemed.

Though they could lift a great deal, airboats could never move faster than a good stagecoach or clipper. Their primary advantage was that they rose far above pirates, bandits, and even storms. Hence, if you wanted to cross the Boiling Sea to Regalious, an airboat was your only option.

At one of the airdock's various loading stations, a wagon rolled into a zone marked, "No Parking," pulled by a donkey with other things on its mind. For a while, the canvas covering the rear of the wagon shook and bulged with unidentifiable activity and, after a time, a man hopped from the wagon and looked around shiftily.

The man was Azron, though you'd have to look twice to realize it. Gone were the long greasy coat and the peak-less woolen hat, replaced by finery fashionable with the richer gentlemen of the Empire. A gaudy blue waistcoat was worn baggy over a white shirt obviously tailored for a shorter man. Long black trousers didn't quite reach his ankles and shiny black shoes pinched his toes. The whole thing was pulled together with a silken red necktie that looked uncomfortable on Azron's bird-like neck. His lank hair was pulled and oiled into a precise center parting; perhaps the only part of the thief that wasn't crooked.

Azron, seeing that the coast was clear, motioned for the wagon's other occupant to come out from hiding. After a while, he motioned again.

"Look, are you coming or what?" he hissed.

"No," replied a muffled voice.

"Don't be silly!" Azron chided. "You knew we had to be in disguise!"

A man's head emerged from the wagon. On it were a women's wig, make-up, and a ribbon-laden hat.

"I don't see why I have to be the wife," said Bip, sharply.

"I already told you," replied Azron. "I'm allergic to lace."

Bip fully exited the wagon to reveal a long, flowing gown that engulfed most of the shorter man's frame. Oddly, with his pale features and light beard, Bip made a halfway convincing woman.

"You'll have to lose the specs," said Azron. "They don't go with your eye-shadow."

"Oh, shut up," Bip said testily. "I'm not taking my glasses off."

"Yeah, all right, keep your wig on."

"You're not funny."

"Who's trying to be funny? And will you try to keep your voice effeminate please?"

"Sod off."

The two interlopers walked calmly through the surging crowds of the airdock, all the while keeping an eye out for anyone who might be watching them suspiciously. The goblins had gone to the trouble of constructing new identities for Bip and Azron, but the skimpy disguises wouldn't fool anyone who was looking for them for long, and it wasn't just Tony's thugs they had to worry about—the grim faces of airdock security awaited at every turn.

Still more worrying was the overbearing presence of Imperial Regulators. These lawmen stood around in shadowy corners making no effort to hide their suspicious staring. Dressed entirely in gray, from their leather gloves to their neatly tailored overcoats and top hats, the Regulators drifted through the crowd like specters through fog. The Imperial agents had the right to detain and question anybody they thought suspicious and, being renowned for their brutality, were feared greatly on both sides of the Boiling Sea. Around their waists, they wore sturdy leather holsters where flintlock pistols rested with threatening readiness.

Bip had been horrified to learn what flintlocks actually were—devices designed entirely to explosively launch a piece of metal through a human target. ("I suppose it's like being stabbed," Azron had said. "Only less personal.") The possession of flintlocks or gunnery of any kind was rare in the Free Countries, and only Imperial agents were allowed to wear them openly in public. And wear them openly they did, flaunting their pistols with a boyish pride that certain psychologists would have a lot to say about. Bip watched the Regulators carefully, not liking the steely smirks they uniformly wore. Despite the elegance of their clothing, the Regulators had a thuggishness about them that rivaled the lowliest hoodlum. Bip knew instinctively that they were best avoided.

Arm in arm, Bip and Azron made their way to Passenger Terminal One, a terminal designed for the transportation of people with enough money to make the wheels of bureaucracy turn a little faster than usual. According to their papers, Bip and Azron were Mr. and Mrs. Cornwall Thatcher, wealthy landowners from somewhere called

Panthalus who had property interests in the Free Countries. Bip was unsure of what had happened to the real Mr. and Mrs. Cornwall Thatcher, but was grateful for the expedience of departure their wealth and station was sure to grant. The two fugitives joined their designated departure queue, filled with elegantly dressed and comfortably fat men and women, all waiting to have their papers and tickets inspected by the boarding security staff.

"Just keep calm, dear," said Azron, noticing the way Bip glanced nervously around the terminal.

"Don't call me 'dear,'" Bip replied testily.

"Darling?"

"No! Sod off!"

A few of the other boarders in the queue, a wealthy looking family with snooty countenances, began to turn curious glances at the bickering couple. A fat lady directly behind them in the queue cleared her throat pompously.

"Now, now, pumpkin." Azron smirked. "Let's not cause a scene."

"You utter bastard," Bip mumbled.

"Sorry?"

"I said, 'Yes, dear,'" said Bip.

"That's more like it."

***

HANDEN STRIKE WALKED through the rock lands. His lips were papery from constant thirst and a film of sweat clung desperately to his brow. The heat was beginning to affect his thinking, he knew. He had been daydreaming, vividly imagining that he was still in chronostatic sleep, watching Bersch from the comfortable coolness of the *Sentinel*. As he watched, he had been able to see the progress he was making down on the planet surface, represented by a dotted red line that twisted and circled but never went straight. He had grown more and more frustrated watching the red line continuously diverting, until he'd snapped awake, remembering where he was. He had reached the fourth of the Spine Islands, which wasn't as rich and green as the first, but thankfully didn't contain as many ravenous alligator people.

So far, the island had been mostly barren wilderness: flat, baked, and eerily quiet and still under a wide, open sky. Not that Handen minded. He'd take eerily quiet over huge, roaring alligatormen any day. Despite the heat and thirst, he was presently happy with the latest island. There had been no monsters, no evil cults, and no damsels in distress for a good few days now. In fact, there had been no one at all. He was beginning to wonder if the island was uninhabited. He fervently hoped that it was.

"Excuse me," came a voice from behind him.

Handen groaned inwardly and turned around. Behind him stood a tall and pretty girl. Her skin was dark and her eyes bright. Her hair, a golden-brown, was short and fluffy in an attractive kind of way. She was wrapped against the barren winds in a blanket that concealed almost all of her body. She seemed slightly hunched, as though cold.

Handen searched the empty landscape, wondering where the girl could have come from and what she wanted. Judging by his past experiences, he felt that there were probably only two real options. "You're not a damsel in distress, are you?" he said wearily.

"Hardly," huffed the maiden and with a sudden shrug, dropped her blanket to the sandy floor, revealing her naked body underneath. For a moment, Handen thought the vision of beauty that stood before him was too good to be true. Then he realized that it was. The maiden had a heavenly body, with creamy skin that smoothed over a toned and marvelous torso peaked by soft, round breasts. The effect was marred slightly by the large talons that protruded where her forearms and feet should have been and the huge feathery wings that grew from her shoulder blades.

The girl was quite obviously a harpy: half woman and half bird of prey. Though he had never seen one before, Handen had heard of their reputation as fearsome hunters and merciless fighters. His libido had a brief and torrid struggle with his survival instincts, his gaze shifting ceaselessly from breast to talon. Eventually and predictably, the former Hostility Advisor's survival instinct proved stronger. He readied his hand at his whip and prepared for battle. And then paused. With a heavy weariness, he lowered his hand, allowing it to slump by his side with an indifferent shrug.

"You know what?" he said. "I'm tired. Damn tired of this. Seems I can't go anywhere without somebody wanting a piece of me. Well, you can find your fun elsewhere. I'm not interested."

The harpy opened her mouth to speak.

"No!" interrupted Handen.

"But—"

Handen flapped his hand dismissively. "Not interested. Goodbye."

The jaded adventurer walked off into the wilderness, muttering under his breath and kicking at the rocks under his feet.

The harpy watched him go, then sighed, flapping her wings absent-mindedly in the harsh wilderness breeze. Maybe she had been too upfront with the handsome stranger, but it was getting harder and harder to find a date on the Spine Islands, especially when everyone assumed you were a fearsome hunter and merciless fighter. Well, whatever. The stranger obviously hadn't been interested in chicks.

BIP AND AZRON moved slowly along the queue, the drudging progress of the passengers dictated by the various ineptitudes of the bored-looking boarding staff. An air of testiness saturated the atmosphere of the terminal. It seemed that even the more privileged airboat travelers had a difficult time surviving the sheer mundanity of flight delay.

It had been a long while since anyone in the queue had talked. The futility of complaint had been realized long ago, so now the terminal reverberated with the sound of hundreds of worn-out people breathing hard through their nostrils.

Suddenly, the relative silence was broken by the sharp clump of booted feet. Bip turned to notice a large contingent of men in black leather entering the terminal and fanning out amongst the crowds. He gulped. Topman's men had arrived.

Bip nudged Azron.

"I know," muttered Azron. He spoke without seeming to move his lips, staring straight ahead. "Keep calm and don't stare at them."

Bip tried hard not to look but couldn't help shifting his gaze to the figures in black who now wandered through the terminal. He saw one of the men talking to an Imperial Regulator, showing him a piece of paper with two sketches on it. Bip knew deep down that the sketches were of Azron and himself. He gulped again as one of the Regulators pointed in the direction of the boarding queue they were standing in.

The queue continued to move forward at its ponderous plod as Topman's guards began pacing the line, carefully examining the faces of the waiting passengers. If one of the guards were able to get a look at the two disguised fugitives, they would be recognized for sure.

Bip nudged Azron in the ribs again.

"I know," said the thief. "Stay calm and get ready to follow my lead."

The Diamond Geezer took a small glass phial from a pocket inside his waistcoat, and with his long, delicate fingers, began to unscrew the cap. When this was done, he put the flask behind his back and turned it upside down in one quick movement. Azron secreted the flask back in his waistcoat just as Bip noticed the large puddle of clear, oily liquid that now oozed on the floor directly behind them.

"Cooking oil," whispered Azron. "Very handy in the right circumstances."

The queue moved forward slowly, and Bip, with unusually clear foresight, thought of the fat lady directly behind them. Azron grabbed his arm and walked him hurriedly forward just as a piercing wail and thunderous crash erupted from behind them.

All eyes turned to the fat lady as she struggled on the suddenly slippery floor, roaring with furious humiliation, a whirl of heels and petticoat. Several staff ran over to assist the clamorous woman, and they themselves began sliding in the oily liquid as they endeavored to lift the large lady from the floor. The whole terminal, their minds starved of activity, began to watch the flurrying efforts to right the fallen woman with some interest. So distracted were they that no one, not even Topman's guards and the Imperial Regulators, noticed when Bip and Azron slipped in at the head of the queue. Azron placed their papers and tickets in front of the clerk. "Two for the 3:45 to the mainland, please," he said, chirpily. And it really was as simple as that.

16

Mr. Random

Bip relaxed. The interior of the airboat was quite luxurious compared to the slapdash countenance of its exterior. Large, comfortable chairs stood in cozy rows down the length of the passenger compartment, while gorgeous flight attendants walked ceaselessly up and down the aisles in between. The constant hum of the engines that powered both the propulsion fans and the hydrosac were strangely lulling, and Bip felt his eyes grow heavier as the airboat floated softly into the sky.

He had felt a bit nervous about flying at first as they had risen up to the waiting airboat in one of the balloon cranes but had been soothed by constantly smiling flight attendants and a sky captain whose voice had exuded more confidence than you would have thought possible in one man. Besides, the alternative to boarding the airboat would have been staying in the boarding lounge, where Topman's guards would undoubtedly have found them. Bip had been more impressed than terrified when the airboat cast off. He had watched with interest as the airdock and Port Town had decreased in size until they became an unimportant speck on a vista of green.

Azron had put up a fuss when boarding, but only because someone had told him he wouldn't be able to smoke for the entire journey. His outrage had been subdued, however, when the Sky Captain had taken him aside and told him that unsupervised naked flame on an airboat could result in the explosive death of everyone on board.

They had, thankfully, been able to discard their disguises and don their normal clothes once they had reached the balloon cranes, so Bip was able to sit comfortably for the journey and drop his pantomimic pretense at femininity. And now they had been rolling along in the skies for some hours, looking down at roaring rivers suddenly tamed to thin, delicate lines and massive mountain ranges made fragile by perspective. After a long time, they had eventually reached the end of the Free Countries and floated over a sea that seemed to constantly shimmer and boil.

"It's the Boiling Sea," Azron said when Bip inquired. "It's the reason we have to travel by airboat. You'd be torn to pieces if you tried to sail through it."

Bip gazed down at the swirling currents, the raging storm calmed by distance. He felt oddly peaceful.

Two days passed, and the airboat was well over the Boiling Sea. Despite the comfort of the passenger deck and the access to the exercise deck (a large, empty room designed specifically for walking up and down in), the passengers were growing restless. Bip, however, was enjoying the quiet and was still quite thrilled by the miniature panorama that spread below. He allowed himself to lie back in his comfortable chair and loosen up. Next to him, Azron fidgeted in his sleep, his nicotine cravings affecting his dreams. Bip felt the world turn soft around him as the constant lull of the engines carried his consciousness away.

Suddenly he snapped awake. There was a subtle wrongness in the air that he couldn't quite put his finger on. He looked around the darkened passenger deck. He couldn't tell how long he had been sleeping, but the sunlight outside the window had left, and most of the passengers seemed to be asleep. The nagging feeling continued to gnaw at some part of his subconscious. It was a feeling that he had misplaced or forgotten something, or that something didn't quite fit right in the world. He felt as if he'd woken up in a nightmare.

His eyes flicking nervously from side to side, Bip searched around the passenger compartment, hoping to verify the source of his unease. It did not take him long to find it. Standing in one of the aisles was a figure that clearly did not belong in the passenger compartment, a spindly, jagged figure silhouetted against the dull cabin lamps. He wore a somber black suit with a thin bootlace tie, but these were the only things normal about the stranger. His face resembled a goblin's in shape, though his ears were shorter and more pointed, and his nose and chin were both long and sharp, flanked by eyes that were deep set and yellow. But what set him aside from anyone Bip had ever seen was the deep red tone of his skin and the two small but spiky-looking horns protruding from his forehead. The stranger was looking directly at him. He smiled, revealing a mouth full of razor-sharp metal teeth.

"You're a dream," murmured Bip.

The stranger's face twisted in irritation. "I thought we'd got past that last time?" he said, in a voice that was far more elegant than the features it came from. Bip frowned, wondering what the creature meant.

"You know, you really are a persistent little bugger," said the creature, looking at his nails in a distracted fashion. "I'd assumed that the yeti would finish you off, but no, you survive. Then you had the audacity to breeze through the Cold Ocean like it was the easiest thing in the world. And then—*then*—alone in one of the most dishonest cities on the planet, you completely fail to be killed by a murderous assailant. What will we do with you, ay?"

"Who are you?" said Bip.

"You can call me Mr. Random," said the creature. "Pleased to meet you. You and I are going to be seeing a lot more of each other from here on in."

Something about Mr. Random's voice was scratching at Bip's memory. "I've met you before, haven't I?" he said.

"Very observant," said Mr. Random.

"You were the seagull!" exclaimed Bip. A few of the passengers began to look in his direction. Somebody made a harsh *shhh* noise.

"Don't worry about them," said Mr. Random. "They can't see me. Only you can see me, Bip." The creature began to walk toward the traveler.

"What do you want?" said Bip, a slight tremble in his voice betraying his bravado.

"Simple, Bippy-boy, simple. I want you to go home. Go home and forget all this saving the world business."

"I...I can't. I couldn't do that," said Bip.

The creature clucked its forked tongue. "You've been lucky so far, Bip, that's all. Lucky. Do you really think your luck will hold out?"

"I don't understand," said Bip. "Why would you want to stop me?"

Mr. Random looked at his nails again, pointy white stubs on the end of fiendishly long fingers. "You know how some people believe they have guardian angels, Bip?"

Bip nodded.

"Well, think of me as the exact opposite. Sort of an anti-guardian, if you like. It's my job to make sure that everything goes as badly as possible for you."

"What do you mean?" said Bip.

"Well, for instance, who do you think tipped off Tony's guards as to your whereabouts back at the airdock?"

"That was you?"

"Too right!" said Mr. Random. "A whisper here, a whisper there. You'd be surprised by what you can achieve."

Suddenly, realization gave Bip a swift kick to the head as he remembered something from his training days. "You!" he exclaimed. "You're one of the Discordance!"

The creature grinned its horrible metal grin. "Yes," it said. "And I'm warning you to turn back now." The creature leaned in over Bip until he could see a dull red glint in each yellow eye and smell burning meat on the creature's breath. "Turn back or die slow," it said.

"You don't scare me," said Bip (though a pressing need in his bladder was telling him differently). "You know what I think? I don't think you can even touch me! If you could hurt me yourself, you would have killed me by now."

Mr. Random stepped back and stared at Bip with a smirking appraisal. "Yes, you're right—I can't touch you. But I don't need to, not when I can get others to do it for me."

As if on cue, a flight attendant began walking down the aisle, a tray of hot coffee in her hands and a cheery grin still plastered across her face despite the lateness of the hour.

Mr. Random waited until the attendant was walking past and whispered something in her ear. The flight attendant looked confused for a moment, then dropped the tray of coffee right in Bip's lap. Bip's screech awakened most of the passengers, who began looking about with muzzy alarm.

"Oh my gosh!" said the attendant. "I'm so sorry, sir—I don't know what happened!"

"It's okay," said Bip, through teeth clenched in pain. "It's okay, I'll be fine."

"I'll get you a towel," said the attendant, and ran off down the aisle.

"You see?" said Mr. Random, laughing. "The poor girl doesn't have an aggressive bone in her body, but it was the work of a second to get her to scald you."

Bip gritted his teeth against the stream of swear words that fought to get out of his mouth.

"Do yourself a favor, Bippy-boy," said Mr. Random. "Go back. Go back or die slow." Then the creature vanished with a pop.

"Utter, utter bastard!" screeched Bip.

"What?" said Azron, as he snapped out of his deep slumber.

MR. RANDOM FLOATED on the currents of the sky as he watched the airboat drift into the distance. In truth, he was worried by Bip's luck. Against Mr. Random's interference, people generally didn't make it very far at all, but Bip seemed to be holding strong. Still, there were plenty of hazards between here and the capital, and there were a million things that could go wrong. Mr. Random was here to make sure that each and every one of them did.

17

Regalious

Situated on the seventh of the Spine Islands is a solitary mountain, a pile of precariously balanced stones set uneasily in the surrounding desert. From this distance, you might think a strong breeze could blow it over, so narrow the mountain seems against the flatness of the plains. And though it does seem to creak alarmingly in the dust storm that rages continuously below, the mountain has stood since the dawn of creation, a pinnacle of permanence in the shifting landscape around it. The very top of the mountain was perfectly flat, giving it a cue-like shape that had earned it the name Lightning Rod.

Atop the mountain, sitting cross-legged on a rock and lost in deep meditation, was a Mahrai warrior of the Thunder Tribe. His uniform of a ragged loincloth and a headdress made of various animal bones was his only barrier against the chill wind that whistled ceaselessly in the high altitude.

His name was DaoGryn, which in his tribal tongue translated as "wolf bringer of death," a fact that might have got a few drinks brought for him had he ever frequented any bars. DaoGryn was the greatest warrior his tribe had ever known, unbeatable in unarmed combat and fearless in the face of any danger. It was for this reason that the spirits had made him Guard of the Pass, the highest honor known to the Thunder Tribe. DaoGryn had accepted the honor willingly, though it meant his exile to the Lightning Rod, where he would spend the rest of his days guarding the knowledge of the Pass. He sat, as he sat every day, attuning his mind to the world around him. He had applied his war paint over his dark skin that morning, as he did every morning, even though he hadn't seen a soul in over three years. However, he knew beyond a shadow of a doubt that the one day he decided to forgo his war paint would be the one day when he'd have visitors. So, he sat atop the Lightning Rod, painted and ready, waiting for the day when someone would challenge the Pass.

DaoGryn's ears pricked at the sound of sliding stone, followed by a grunt and a thump. He turned to see a man haul himself over the mountain's edge and waited, allowing the stranger to get some of his breath back. The climb to the top of the Lightning Rod was a tough one, he knew. He had made the climb himself over three years ago. DaoGryn took a moment to study the newcomer. There was something unusual about the man's aura, something older than the man himself. Something that had been around. DaoGryn put aside his musings. There was only one true way to know somebody.

"You seek knowledge of the Pass," said the Mahrai.

"Yes," said the stranger.

"Then you know there is a test?"

"Yes," said the stranger.

"Tell me," said DaoGryn, "what is your name?"

"Is this part of the test?"

"No. That would be too easy." The Mahrai warrior grinned.

"My name is Handen Strike," said Handen.

"And I am DaoGryn, wolf bringer of death, chosen one and profound warrior, guardian of the knowledge of the Pass."

"Well, Mr. Pass," said Handen impatiently, "I believe you mentioned something about a test?"

DaoGryn smiled. "I think the test of mind is not your preferred path, yes? My feelings tell me you are a man of action."

"Your feelings tell you correctly."

"Then the test of the fist is more to your preference?"

"Damn straight," said Handen, cracking his knuckles loudly.

DaoGryn looked closely at the newcomer again, attuning his senses to the man's natural energies. Handen's aura was certainly unusual, bearing scars that didn't show on flesh, telling tales that Handen himself had never told. DaoGryn realized something in a flash, something he had only heard about in the fables of his elders.

"You have the curse of the hero about you," he said.

"Is that what they call it?" said Handen casually. "I thought it was just rotten luck." He rolled his neck, producing a series of loud popping noises. "Now are we going to fight or what?"

DaoGryn rose from his rock and studied the adventurer for a while. "Well, hero, your quest ends here," he said. "No one has ever beaten me."

"There's a first time for everything," replied Handen.

The Mahrai flexed and rotated his narrowly muscled shoulders. "Remove your weapons and prepare your soul."

DaoGryn watched as Handen first threw his whip and sword to the ground, then an assortment of weighted throwing knives and daggers, then a few clubs, chains and throwing darts, then a small war axe. Finally, he unstrapped a huge beasthunter crossbow from his back and threw it to the floor with a clang.

"Is that everything?" asked DaoGryn.

Handen looked thoughtful and shook his left boot. A few rogue throwing knives clattered to the ground.

"Let's do it," he said, easing his body into a ready position.

Without warning, DaoGryn seemed to explode into a whirlwind of fist and foot, launching attacks at Handen that even the quick-handed adventurer had trouble deflecting. Handen Strike quickly found himself on the defensive, blocking with arm and knee blows that were almost too quick for the eye. The Mahrai warrior seemed to defy gravity, landing blows with limbs that should have been supporting his weight, throwing punches from seemingly impossible angles. After a short while, DaoGryn landed his first proper hit, breaking Handen's guard with a sweeping kick and following through with a lightning back-knuckle. While Handen was temporarily stunned by the blow, the Mahrai followed the momentum of his spin and delivered a devastating double-fisted punch that sent the former Hostilities Advisor staggering backward, nearly but not quite toppling to the ground.

Handen shook his head and readied his guard again, shifting his weight and stance slightly now he had some idea of his opponent's strength and speed—both far greater than he had anticipated.

With a blurry swiftness, DaoGryn flipped onto his hands and launched himself feet-first into an attack, legs whirring in a flurry of kicks as he arced through the air. Handen managed to roll his body backward, catching the last of DaoGryn's kicks in his palms and pushing the offending leg upward hard, hoping to put the warrior off balance. DaoGryn merely used the force of Handen's block to flip himself backward in midair, darting out with a swift kick at the apex of his flight, catching Handen with a weak but unexpected blow to the chin. Handen was surprised by the kick, but by no means felled. He launched from his crouching position and attacked before the Mahrai had time to erect a proper defense. Handen's bulkier frame lent him an advantage as he ploughed his fists into the smaller man's torso three times in blurred succession, forcing DaoGryn to shift his guard to ward off the blows. Handen was already one step ahead of the response, however, and landed a brutal head-butt on the warrior's nose. The unexpected force sent him sprawling backward.

The Mahrai looked momentarily shocked, wiping dumbly at the blood on his nose and then, as if remembering himself, he oiled smoothly back into his fighting stance. Handen waited for the attack. Though DaoGryn had regained his composure, Handen had seen the brief look of rage in his opponent's eye. He had a feeling the next attack would be more furious than anything he'd tried previously. He was right.

DaoGryn first flipped backward onto his hands, then sprang farther back onto a jutting rock. He had barely touched the rock with his feet when he was suddenly flying straight toward the adventurer, fist extended before him and a high battle cry erupting from his throat. But Handen had banked on an elaborate charge and, rather than defending, this time rolled forward toward the warrior. Handen used the momentum of his roll to launch himself upward fist first, catching the leaping Mahrai in the chest with a rising uppercut that was equal parts luck and skill. DaoGryn sailed through the air, his battle cry cut off with a surprised *whoof!* as the wind was forced from his lungs. He hit the ground hard but sprang immediately to his feet.

DaoGryn was furious. He had never in his adult life been knocked down by an opponent. He breathed heavily as he tried to dismiss the pain in his chest and face. Then, almost as if someone had hit some sort of switch in the warrior's body, he calmed and focused, his breathing returning to normal, a faraway look in his eye.

Handen watched and waited for the next attack. He grew increasingly uneasy as the Mahrai stared straight into nothingness, his features totally impassive. The air around the warrior began to shimmer, a light wind whipping around him. Dust from the mountaintop floor began to rise and sway in the personalized gale. The Mahrai fighter began to emit a low battle cry, its volume and intensity rising steadily.

Handen readied himself, sensing something deeper at work in his opponent's body than mere strength of muscle. He knew with dread certainty that the next attack would be the pinnacle of DaoGryn's skill. All he could do was hope he was strong enough and quick enough to defend against it. He dug his feet into the ground beneath him and held his arms out, ready for combat.

Without warning, thunder boomed in the air as DaoGryn's battle cry reached a crescendo, and with amazing speed, the warrior leaped through the air, dust exploding in his wake as he rocketed toward Handen. At the last possible second before impact, DaoGryn struck out with a devastating kick.

To Handen's credit, he did manage to block the kick, crossing his arms over his chest as the blow connected. Unfortunately, it wasn't enough. He heard a loud snap as one of his arms broke and felt the breath rocket from his lungs as the kick drove into his ribs. The sheer force of the attack sent him flying through the air and over the lip of the mountain. The wind whipped away his scream as he plummeted the countless feet to the rocks below. Then there was no sound but the whistle of the endless dust storms, gently but persistently eroding the base of the Lightning Rod. DaoGryn fell to his knees, his head spinning as oxygen flooded back into his body. He had put all his energy into his last attack and was now too weak to move.

He was relieved he had been able to beat the stranger, but also felt a brief sadness. The fight had been his greatest yet, and he thought it unlikely he would ever face an opponent as worthy as the one he had just defeated. Tomorrow he would return to his tribe, he thought, and take a well-deserved holiday. The Spirits could guard their own mystic knowledge for a change.

With great effort, the Mahrai warrior managed to stumble back to his rock. He returned to his meditation, thankful for the rest.

He meditated for some hours before his concentration was broken once again by the sound of sliding rock. He looked to the mountain lip with a growing sense of dread as first one gloved hand then the other grasped the edge. DaoGryn couldn't suppress a gasp of shock as Handen Strike pulled himself onto the mountaintop once more.

The adventurer stood before the warrior, breathing hard, a look of jaded fury in his eyes.

"I'll tell you what," said DaoGryn after a while, "why don't I just tell you about the Pass, yes?"

Handen nodded. "That would save some time."

"If you travel northeast from here, you'll come across a cave entrance by two large burra bushes. If you follow the cave through, turning left at every fork, you'll eventually get to the mainland."

Handen stood staring for a while. "That's it?" he said, after a time. "That's the knowledge of the Pass?"

The Mahrai shrugged.

"I climbed all the way up here so you could tell me about a bloody cave?" said Handen.

DaoGryn shrugged again. "It's the Pass," he said, simply. "I've just told you the knowledge of it."

Handen shook his head and began walking away.

"I should warn you, though, hero," DaoGryn called after him. "The

Pass is home to beasts of demonic proportions and monsters born from the very heart of darkness."

The immortal turned to face the warrior, a cynical look on his face. "I think I'll be all right, don't you?" he said, then stepped off the edge of the mountain.

DaoGryn looked thoughtfully for a while at the space where Handen had been. He wasn't sure if he had won or lost the fight and eventually decided to chalk it up as a draw. After all, anyone who could fall off a mountain then climb back up and ask for directions couldn't really be classed as a typical opponent.

THERE WERE SMALLER piles of rocks at the bottom of the mountain, all quite unremarkable compared to the towering shape of the Lightning Rod, but each fairly impressive in its own way. Overall, it was a peaceful scene at the north side of the mountain's base, sheltered as it was from the sweltering sun and constant dust storms, silent in the hardpan desert.

The silence was broken by the faint sound of screaming, which grew louder and louder until it was cut off by an abrupt splat as the body of Handen Strike impacted with one of the aforementioned piles of rocks. There was a brief rain of blood followed by the silence the mountain base was accustomed to.

After about thirty minutes, the adventurer stood up and dusted himself down. All traces of having fallen five hundred feet onto some pointy rocks had vanished. The fall had been extremely painful, but Handen was in a hurry. He had taken far too long to cross the Spine Islands and, now that he had directions to the mainland, he had no intention of staying on the accursed islands any longer than he had to.

He was getting closer to his goal. He had faced more challenges and opponents than any one man should have to. He was going to let nothing stand in his way.

THE AIRBOAT SAILED FAR above the unvarying tantrum of the Boiling Sea, floating through the peaceful heights, lolling along with packs of lazy clouds like ancient herbivores. It passed over the aptly named Spine Islands, a thin row of vertebrae linking the two continents in a tether of jagged lands. Finally, it reached the shores of the mainland—the continent of Regalious, the heart and home of the Empire.

Bip looked out of the window as the airboat descended, awestruck as once again geographical features expanded back into all-consuming realities rather than far-away dreams.

THE AIRBOAT LANDED JUST as dawn was breaking at Panthalus Airdock. To the east, the sky was a promising shade of turquoise, crisscrossed with thin strips of salmon-stained clouds. The dawn light was gray but not cold, and in the distance, it was possible to make out the towering white peaks of the nearby city of Panthalus.

Passing through the security checks once they had landed was far less of an ordeal than it had been in Port Town. Passengers milled around, awaiting coaches and trams that would take them into the city proper. They reveled in the fresh air and solid ground, glad to be away from the airboat they had been cooped up on for nearly three days. It was going to be a clear morning, warm and pleasant, a fresh welcome from a new land.

Azron smoked furiously, chaining to make up for days without nicotine. A look of deep satisfaction smoothed over the thief's sharp features.

Bip sat on his rucksack, a faint grin hanging delicately beneath his nose as he surveyed the new continent. He felt a real sense of progress about his journey and was pleased to be preparing for travel again. With Brian by his side and sturdy walking boots comfortable on his feet, Bip was feeling an excitement he hadn't experienced since first leaving Kaneq. He missed his hat, though. Even though this new climate had forced him to abandon many of his overcoats, he still felt insecure without his traveling hat.

He lifted his head and breathed deeply of the clear dawn air. He noticed that Azron was doing the same, though a cigarette filtered the process somewhat.

"Where to next, do you think?" said Bip.

Azron was looking out over the horizon. "I think your best bet is the city, mate. Plenty of people there. You can start finding out things, build up some contacts, make your way east to the capital from city to city, like." He blew a small river of cigarette smoke into the cool dawn.

"Okay, then," said Bip. "We'll just hop onto one of those trams, then. There should be one fairly soon."

Azron turned to look at his accomplice. "No 'we' about it, guv. I'm heading south for smaller towns, see how things work around here, get my bearings and work my way up, sort of thing."

Bip gaped momentarily. "You're not coming with me?" he said.

"Sorry, buddy. It's been a blast and all, but it looks like this is where we part company. Different paths and the like, you know."

Bip couldn't help but feel a little downcast. "I was hoping you'd be coming with me. I need all the help I can get."

Azron laughed. "You'll be fine, mate. You survived Port Town, didn't you? Everything from here on in should be a piece of cake."

"Well," said Bip, "I still wish you were coming with me."

Azron turned back to the distant horizon, the look of a die-hard opportunist in his eye. "It's a wide old world, buddy," he said, "but things have a way of working out, you know? I wouldn't be too surprised if we bumped into each other again."

"So this is goodbye, then?" said Bip.

"Not so much goodbye as…see you later," said Azron, and began walking away. He stopped suddenly. "Oh yeah," he muttered, and began rummaging through the pockets of his long coat. From them he pulled a bag of acorns, a bottle of spiritl and a corned beef sandwich. "These belong to you." He grinned.

Bip floundered briefly. "How did you…?"

"Nicked them, didn't I? Nothing personal, mate—it's just what I do. I'm a Diamond Geezer, remember?"

"Yeah. I suppose," said Bip.

"Remember, mate," said the thief, "mugs and muggers, yeah? Don't be a mug." With that, he patted Bip on the cheek and walked into the distance.

Bip watched him go until he was quite far away. Then Azron turned as if remembering something.

"Good luck with saving the world, by the way!" he called.

Bip waved and watched as his only friend in this wide new world disappeared over the horizon.

HANDEN WAITED in the Imperial waiting room, freshly shaved, a ton of road dirt scrubbed from his body, his hair pulled into a severe parting. He stood bolt upright, attired in the finest clothes he had been able to afford. On the wall, a mechanical timepiece, the most intricate piece of technology Handen had seen in centuries, ticked and tocked with graceful formality.

A stiff-necked attendant peered around the chamber door.

"The Emperor will see you shortly," he said.

Handen nodded. He had come halfway across the world. He had traveled for years and fought longer and harder than any man he had heard of. Finally, he had reached his goal. It had taken months of long waits and constant cajoling but, at last, he had been granted an audience with the most powerful man on Bersch.

The jaded adventurer felt his first rush of true excitement for decades. He knew, deep down, that his mission was almost complete.

AND NOW, once again, adjust your perspective. Leave the young man boarding his tram, alone but determined, his delicate chin set firmly as he heads through yet another unknown world. Leave the immortal adventurer who, jaded as he is, still has his mission and his hope. Leave the thief in a foreign land, seeking new and interesting things to steal. Leave an Emperor sitting on a throne of madness, dark whisperings echoing through a twisted consciousness. Readjust your perspective as the cities and countries dwindle and merge and continents blur into oceans. This is the planet of Bersch. Take a good look. It might not be here much longer.

To Be Continued in The Chained Immortal -
Book 2 of The Doomsayer Journeys.
Available Now from Falstaff Books.

If you enjoyed this book and would like to be notified of new releases, appearances, and everything else related to Steve Wetherell, sign up for the newsletter here -
http://eepurl.com/cv5FSj

Acknowledgments

Special thanks to Rebecca Hill for editing the initial publication of this book, and to Graham White for the original cover art.

About the Author

Steve Wetherell is an author, comedy writer and podcast idiot. He regularly writes humorous nonsense on the internet, and cordially invites you to join him. He lives in the English midlands with his wife, kids, and laptop, and his interests include beer, rock music and writing about himself in the third person.

Also by Steve Wetherell

Authors & Dragons - Podcast

Hell's Titties

The Totally Legend of Brandon Thighmaster

The Ballad of Aaron Bezron

Shoot the Dead

Far into the Dark

The Torso Farmer

www.ingramcontent.com/pod-product-compliance
Lightning Source LLC
Chambersburg PA
CBHW032000180726
48283CB00008B/2513